BAYOU WHISPERS

R.B. WOOD

**Let the world know:
#IGotMyCLPBook!**

**Crystal Lake Publishing
www.CrystalLakePub.com**

Cover Design:
Kip Ayers

Interior Layout:
Lori Michelle—www.theauthorsalley.com

Proofread by:
Paula Limbaugh
Roberta Codemo

WELCOME
TO ANOTHER

CRYSTAL LAKE PUBLISHING
CREATION

Join today at www.crystallakepub.com & www.patreon.com/CLF

Welcome to another Crystal Lake Publishing creation.

Thank you for supporting independent publishing and small presses. You rock, and hopefully you'll quickly realize why we've become one of the world's leading publishers of Dark Fiction and Horror. We have some of the best fans for a reason, and hopefully we'll be able to add you to that list really soon.

To follow us behind the scenes (while supporting independent publishing and our authors), be sure to join our interactive community of authors and readers on Patreon (https://www.patreon.com/CLP) for exclusive content. You can even subscribe to all our future releases. Otherwise drop by our website and online store (www.crystallakepub.com/). We'd love to have you.

Welcome to Crystal Lake Publishing Tales from the Darkest Depths.

For Dr. Rachel Geller and Joel Kaplan—great friends who inspire me every day. Thank you for setting me on the right path. I adore you both.

And for Jeannine. Always loved, never forgotten.

PROLOGUE

31 October 2005
Orleans Parish, Louisiana

O N HALLOWEEN NIGHT that year, no little ghosts or goblins wandered the streets in search of candy. No laughter rang out in what was left of the Lower 9th Ward neighborhood. Two months after Katrina had ravaged this place, it still resembled a war zone, covered in debris and stagnant pools of foul-smelling water from the levee breach.

As midnight approached, a young teenager— naked, dirty, covered in mosquito bites, and with a nasty leg wound wrapped in crusted-over grey rags— stumbled from a copse of trees. She was thin, so very thin, weighing barely eighty pounds.

The muddy and cracked streets before her sat dark and empty; human detritus littered the roads and yards, and the skeletons of ruined homes bore unintelligible spray paint that looked more like the desperate scratching of a fluorescent wild beast than symbols from a nameless insurance company or traumatized recovery workers.

It was a city of the dead, a city of the damned.

Right foot, left foot drag. One step at a time. The pain didn't matter. It can't matter.

1

Jeannine had been walking for what felt like forever, almost in a trance, placing one bloody foot in front of the other. Moving forward was the only thing that mattered.

Keep moving. Those white guys might be following. Keep moving.

Right foot, left foot drag.

She walked through glass and rusted nails, around junked appliances and damp, moldy couches. A dog barked once in the distance.

A patrol car sat watch at the end of the street, engine idling. Jeannine approached, fear causing each step to hesitate. The light of a burning cigarette brightened as the occupant of the vehicle, still in shadow, took a long drag.

"Help," croaked Jeannine. Her voice strained, rough. Insects chirped. Frogs called to their mates. No one heard her.

Right foot, left foot drag.

The person in the car took another pull, a dot of orange light flaring, then fading.

"Help!" she called, louder this time. The insects and the frogs stopped. The patrol car's dome light winked on as the door opened.

Jeannine screamed.

She screamed as the cop ran toward her. She screamed as the cop took off his own shirt to wrap around her. She screamed as the cop carried her to the car.

"Jesus H. Christ! Randy, call for an ambulance!" yelled the cop.

The cop's partner, still inside the car, got on the radio.

Jeannine continued to scream until her vocal cords tore. She tasted blood.

BAYOU WHISPERS

"You're safe, honey," said the cop for the seventh time. Jeannine finally heard him.

He stayed with her until the ambulance arrived and then rode with her to the hospital. He spoke to the doctors on her behalf. He sat with her in intensive care while Jeannine, clean for the first time in months, slept. He watched her tossing, turning, and moaning softly.

Randy, the cop's partner, arrived at the hospital. He'd taken care of the paperwork and had brought a po' boy and a coffee. The sandwich was left untouched.

For the next hour, the partners sat a silent vigil over Jeannine.

The first cop must have drifted off because he woke with a start when someone placed a hand on his shoulder.

"Officer Jones?" asked a man in scrubs. "I'm Doctor Broussard. Can we talk outside for a minute?"

The cop looked to his partner and he nodded back at him.

"Go," said Randy. "I'll be here."

Jones followed the doctor into the hallway.

"Officer, we can't find any of . . . " He glanced at a clipboard. " . . . Jeannine's family. I wanted to let you know that in the morning, and assuming she's still stable . . . " The doctor let his words drift off as he swallowed hard.

Jones noticed the man's youth, how inexperienced he must've been before Katrina hit. The doctor looked like some of the baby-faced soldiers Curtis had met during the war—young men, children, really, who grew up quickly in the face of tragedy and death.

Jones put his hand on the doctor's shoulder.

"Yes. Sorry," said Dr. Broussard. "It's been a long couple of months of giving out bad news."

"I understand," said Jones automatically. "Just hit me with it, Doc."

"She . . . Jeannine . . . we are going to have to remove her leg. The infection is too severe and there is gangrene."

"Do what you have to," said Jones impassively.

"But without parental . . . "

"Will the surgery save her life?"

"Yes."

"Take her leg, then." Jones's left eye twitched once.

Doctor Broussard nodded. "I'll need you to sign."

A moment later, Jones returned to Jeannine's room.

"Well?" asked Randy.

Jones slumped into a chair. "They're going to take it in the morning."

Suddenly, Jeannine sat up, ice-blue eyes wide, unblinking.

It was those eyes that had thrown him. This young teen—he'd met her once before the storm. He didn't recognize her at first, as she practically crawled from the bayou, filthy and emaciated. The last time Curtis had seen her—she'd been covered in blood.

She had brown eyes then. He remembered them—unblinking and staring into a nightmare of unimaginable horror.

"Jane Doe" was Jeannine LaRue. Jones was sure being a child of mixed-race parents was hard enough to grow up with in this town, but this young woman had experienced far more and far worse than her fourteen years had prepared her for.

Jones knew who she was now; she had been returned unlike so many of those in the missing persons reports.

The details of so many lost souls broken down into height, weight, and hair color.

"You all right, Jeannine?" he asked.

She looked at Jones, eyes unfocused from the drugs the doctors had pumped into her.

"Papa Nightmare is here!" she said in a frantic whisper. "Papa Nightmare!"

"Shhh. It's all right, honey. You are safe now. I'm here and I won't leave you."

Jeannine blankly looked at Jones. He gently helped her lie back down.

"Right foot, left foot," she muttered as her eyes fluttered once before closing.

The drugs took a lasting hold, and Jeannine's breathing slowed. She spoke occasionally, nonsense words mostly. Jones held her hand for the rest of that night.

"You're safe," he whispered again. "I promise."

ONE

Present Day
St. Dismas Parish

T HE AIR FELT THICK, and Curtis Jones always had trouble breathing this time of year. The rain had followed the sunset, but it couldn't wash away the humidity of summer. The moisture in the air hung like damp towels, causing Jones to work harder for each breath.

It might have been the after-effects of Desert Storm. Or the cigarettes. Or maybe it was the fact he was on the downslope toward sixty. For whatever reason, he should have been at home, taking it easy with a bourbon in hand and a sizzling steak fresh off the grill on a paper plate. Or maybe watching the news. Or one of those Lifetime movies Georgina used to like so much.

He should have been doing anything but driving his classic 1987 Grand National T-Type at seventy-plus miles per hour on the slick tarmacadam of Route 21 South while being chased by two sheriff's deputies in a couple of Ford Explorers. But such was the life of a criminal who dipped his wick in the territory run by Major Tommy Dufresne—whose day job was running the St. Dismas Parish Sheriff's Department.

BAYOU WHISPERS

The irony of being a cop who'd turned to crime, being chased by crooked cops, did not escape Jones. He glanced in his rearview mirror at the SUVs with their bright bulbs flashing blue and red, the rain and the dark evening sky making the flashing lights more ominous. The sirens were going, too, for good measure.

"Boys," he murmured, "you haven't a hope in hell."

Jones was once clean cut like he was sure the boys chasing him were. The Major couldn't stand any man in his department who wasn't sporting a buzz cut and a freshly shaven face. The former cop had always assumed it was because the bastard Major couldn't grow a beard of his own. Though Jones used to look like those boys, those days were long gone. His mussed long grey-white hair, salt-and-pepper goatee, and denim jacket were the exact opposite of what the Major would approve of.

Georgina had liked it though. He smiled at the thought.

Jones hit a straight section of Route 21. He mashed the clutch with one alligator-skinned boot, while easing off the gas with the other long enough to shift into fifth. He turned on the radio, and his smile broadened at the sound of this particular Mardi Gras song. It had been a piece of NOLA he'd always carried with him abroad.

He cranked the volume.

My grandma and your grandma were sittin' by the fire . . .

"Be seeing you boys," said Jones to the rearview mirror.

He red-lined the twin turbos and the old muscle

car was soon at a hundred miles per hour. Foolhardy in these conditions, perhaps. But the deputies broke off pursuit when they realized just how crazy the driver of the black '80s muscle car was. Jones knew they had radios, and they'd be on them now, calling ahead. The Major wouldn't want Jones to get out of St. Dismas Parish—he'd have to fight the city and state cops for Jones if he made it to the next jurisdiction.

It was normally an hour to New Orleans from Curtis' home outside of Bush. A bit more to get to the airport. Curtis was betting he could make it in half that time.

But getting away wasn't the point of his running.

Curtis let the words of the song wash over him. Music, smokes, and a fast car. His grin widened.

The tolls at the causeway to cross Lake Pontchartrain would be where they'd get him. Jones could go around the lake, of course. But that would take time. No, it had to be the causeway. He had to give them that chance to get him, to get them away from everyone else. They'd spring a roadblock at the tolls before he could cross into Orleans Parish and get lost in the city.

Jones had made peace with that. As long as they were focused on him, they'd miss what was important back at home. Oh, they'd get to his double-wide eventually, but by then everything would be cleared out. Or burnt to ash.

By that point, Jeannine would be here. After all this time, he'd actually see her again. At his age, there wasn't a lot that made Curtis anxious. He'd fought in multiple wars, worked as a cop, and now was the head of a group of grumpy old criminals. He'd seen death, and worse. Life was like that—a numbing exercise to the horrors the world could inflict.

But he and Jeannine had fallen out hard. Only a double murder rap could get her to take his calls. He'd made her a promise that he'd failed to deliver on, and he wanted to make it right between them.

Not that he honestly cared anymore about going to prison since his wife Georgina had passed. But the thought of seeing Jeannine again rekindled a sense of responsibility for her. Strange that it would be so after so many years of bad blood. But that was behind them. She was smart, and a lawyer. She would find him a way out of wearing an orange jumpsuit. She'd promised.

Or at least promised to find a way for him to avoid the needle.

Jones knew he was being framed, knew the system was rigged against him. Even his higher-up contact wouldn't help him this time.

But Jeannine . . . she said she would.

The song was roaring as loud as the motor, egging Curtis to drive even faster.

Jones hit the outskirts of Covington and took his foot off the gas. No way his classic would take the turn onto Dismas Parkway at speed. Besides, there was a light. And he always hit the damn things as they were changing from yellow to red.

The Grand National protested at the applied brake, the reining in of its horses. His baby hadn't had a good run in nearly a year. Jones patted the steering wheel affectionately, whispering words of love and encouragement only a true motorhead would understand.

He reached into his breast pocket and pulled out a pack of Marlboro Reds. He slipped one between his lips, tossing the nearly full pack on the seat. He grabbed his Army Ranger Zippo, but never had a chance to light his smoke.

The car was slowing to forty when the headlights illuminated the nail strips in the middle of the road.

No! Too soon!

He slammed both feet on the brake and popped the clutch. But given the wet road, the tires, made more for racing than for stopping, slid on the slick pavement. He turned into the skid, of course, tried to control it, but the car had been going too fast. It hit the nail strips, blowing all four tires.

Jones lost any semblance of control.

Sparks flew from the front left, where the tire had shredded right off the rim.

The Buick's rear end led the momentum-fueled crash, bouncing off a light pole and spinning the car 180 degrees.

Then 360.

720.

Thump!

That's when Jones's car hit the edge of the roadway and rolled over an embankment. What was left of his classic car ended up on its side in a McDonald's parking lot.

Jones blinked a couple of times, then struggled to unsnap his racing harness. Once he'd done that, physics—or, more accurately, gravity—brought him crashing down on the passenger side of the vehicle, which, he supposed, was now the bottom of the car.

Vehicles pulled up to where he and the shattered remains of his Grand National lay. Sirens wailed in the background. The rain fell once more, dripping on his face through the shattered window.

"Fuck," he said. *I'll have to kick out the windshield to get . . .*

"Jonesy," called a voice from outside the wreck. "You ain't dead, are ya?"

"Fuck," said Jones again. This time, he meant the curse. He recognized that voice. A voice from his past. A voice he never thought he'd hear again.

His old partner.

The Major must be desperate to pull Randy out of retirement for this, Jones thought, as he attempted, unsuccessfully, to extract himself from his ruined classic. But his flight and now capture had hopefully bought enough time for his *krewe*—he liked the irony of labeling his band of thieves and rogues after a social organization dedicated to celebratory parades, Carnival, and Mardi Gras—to clear out and regroup at their safe place.

"Nah, Randy, I'm cool," Jones called back from inside the shattered car. "But I'm starving. Could you grab me a Big Mac from the drive-through? And I seemed to have misplaced my smokes."

Flashlights and people approached. Randy's voice directed the effort to extract him. A firetruck pulled up and Jones knew he'd be out from the tangle of metal, glass, and plastic soon enough.

As Jones was pulled from the car, his only thought was: *Why isn't the Major here to gloat? He's been waiting to stick it to me since their deaths. Where the hell is that little bastard?*

Meanwhile, the radio somehow played on.

Jack-a-mo fee-no ai na-ne, Jack-amo fee-na-ne!

TWO

JEANNINE LARUE STOOD outside Stanley's brownstone, shaking in the warm summer rain, holding a useless umbrella . . . She was so upset she hadn't even tried to protect her hair from the incessant drops. The result being that the previous $200 straightening process on her thick, black locks had turned to sodden curls. Trying to fit into the look of the otherwise all-white law firm where she worked was a job in and of itself. Stanley had suggested she'd be more "accepted" with straight hair.

Fuck him.

Fuck all of them.

She had been in courtrooms and jailhouses with murderers, rapists, and some of the evilest human trash the city of New York had ever known. None of them had ever fazed her in the slightest. "Ice Queen" is what the good ole' boys in the office called her behind her back. Her friends called her the same thing to her face.

She liked making the white patriarchy nervous. She liked being the Ice Queen.

But Stanley? That son of a bitch could turn her

12

back into a scared fourteen-year-old with a word or a look. She hated him and his multimillion-dollar home-cum-office.

"Fucking asshole," she said to the brownstone behind her. *Pull it together, girl. Get to the airport. You need to be in New Orleans for Curtis by tonight. You promised. You are the Ice Queen!*

The rain fell harder now, and a chill emerged in the air that hadn't been there a moment earlier. Swift temperature changes caused a twinge of pain where the prosthesis joined what was left of her leg. She balanced the umbrella on her shoulder and pulled out her phone to call an Uber when she noticed there was no signal. She tried to wave down a passing taxi, but the guy at the wheel cruised right by, ignoring the non-white-skinned girl in this pasty, rich neighborhood.

"Great. Fuck you, too," she called after it.

Stanley had once suggested that she try to pass as a tanned white power-attorney. But New York knew a non-white girl when it saw one. Sure, things were diverse here, people of every shape and color intermingling in the melting pot of the city.

But the undercurrent of racism was always there.

"It is the only way you'll be successful," Stanley had said. "They'll never say it to your face, but they'll look down on you because of your heritage."

My heritage, she thought. The only stories about her heritage she knew were the weird tales of Voodoo and magic her Nana had told her. Jeannine had thought of them as fairy tales. Or bedtime stories that Nana had made up.

Until recently, she remembered little of her childhood before Katrina. But things were coming to her in dreams, dreams she remembered. First, it was the image of Nana's smile. And then she remembered the fact that Nana was black and so proud and happy to be who she was. She remembered Nana doing her hair, telling her stories of family.

That's when she tried to pull away from Stanley. He'd been molding her into someone that fit *his* idea of success.

Jeannine wanted to be herself. Wanted to be happy. Maybe the rain ruining her hair was finally washing some of the fake away.

She'd have to learn how to care for her hair the way it was, curls and all.

A horn sounded, and she looked up to see a very different cab—an old NYC taxi. All rounded corners, black fenders, yellow doors, and gigantic whitewall tires. Hell, it even had wooden running boards.

"You look like you could use a lift, ma'am," said the cabbie—a thirtyish black man wearing sunglasses and a newsy hat pulled low. He smiled, showing perfectly white teeth.

It was at that moment that the umbrella, perched precariously on Jeannine's shoulder, took off as a gust of wind ripped it from her wet hands. It bounced off the hood of a car and was across the street in the blink of an eye.

"Fuck!" said Jeannine.

The cabbie tutted. "Heaters on in the cab, ma'am. Why don't you let me take you to where you need to be?"

Even though Jeannine was becoming soaked, she hesitated. Something felt—strange.

BOOM! Thunder echoed around the Brooklyn brownstones.

Hell, the Yankees have retro uniforms, she thought. *What's wrong with retro cabs?*

She hurried to open the back door, muscled in her carry-on, and tossed in her briefcase. She heard a thump.

"Ma'am, there is a saxophone in the back seat," said the cabbie over his shoulder. "If you would be so kind as to be gentle with her. I have a gig later, and Ms. Maxine gets all kinds o' fussy if she's knocked around."

Jeannine offered up a half-assed apology as she struggled to climb into the old car.

"Kennedy airport," she said. "Delta terminal."

"Idlewild. Yes, ma'am," replied the cabbie with a tip of his hat, and they were off.

She wasn't really listening. She was replaying the conversation with Stanley, amazed that he, even now, had such power over her emotions.

The wipers on the car were unusually loud and pushed the rain off the windshield as if the water was offering some sort of offense to the classic automobile simply by touching the glass.

Thump-thwack! Thump-thwack!

Jeannine's cellphone rang. She looked at the number, hesitated, then answered.

"What is it, Stanley?"

Jeannine listened for a moment.

"I'm going to stop you there, Stanley. You're not going to change my mind, and . . . hello? Hello?"

Thump-thwack! Thump-thwack!

The cab continued on its way, wipers sounding like gunshots as they swept the deluge from the glass.

"Hello? Damn, what's wrong with this thing?" Jeannine looked down at her phone. Once again, it had no signal.

"Was that yo' man?" asked the cabbie.

"Oh God, no . . . he's . . . my therapist, to be honest."

The driver looked at Jeannine via the old, oval rearview mirror. "Oh?"

She bristled. *Why are all men such assholes?*

"I'm an attorney," she said, emphasizing her title. "I deal with the dregs of society every goddamn day. Sometimes . . . it gets to me."

The cabbie chuckled. "I love seeing the women-folk doin' a man's job—not that there's anything wrong with that," he added hurriedly as he studied Jeannine's frown in the rearview. "Gives me hope for the future, is all."

Jeannine raised her phone to make another call, this time to Curtis, but it still felt strange to just call him after all this time—and there was something about her driver. Something in the way he spoke, maybe, or in that ever-present smile of his. She somehow felt comfortable with this stranger, and that in itself piqued her interest.

She put her cell phone in her coat pocket.

"Why are you driving around in such an old car? It's got to be a classic. Should be in a museum or something."

"Well, little lady, this car is like me. Hates to sit idle. Hates not to be doin' what she was made for. She's like my horn you almost flattened back there."

Jeannine's cheeks flushed. "I really am sorry about that."

"Oh, you don't need to apologize to me, ma'am," replied the cabbie. "But Ms. Maxine, she will not sing for me tonight if she's in a mood, see. But if you apologize to her, that'll make her feel better. Then we'll all feel better. *Tu comprends?*"

Jeannine rolled her eyes. "Oh, for fu . . . I'm not apologizing to a saxophone!"

"You'll feel better. I promise. You dig?" He smiled at her in the rearview mirror.

What is it with this guy? Why am I even talking to him? Jeannine sighed. "Okay. But if you tell anyone, I *am* a lawyer." She looked at the worn and scuffed case. It was covered in tan canvas with frayed, medium-brown leather piping along the edges. Faded tourist stickers from cities around the U.S. decorated the canvas. There were scratches and tears fixed with yellowing tape. Chipped gold letters under the handle spelled out "Easy Street."

This case has seen better days. Maybe the driver, too.

Jeannine sighed again and said, "I'm sorry, Ms. Maxine."

"There! Don't you feel better now?" asked the cabbie, and laughed.

Jeannine laughed with him. The tension that followed the meeting with Stanley melted away. "I actually do feel better. Thank you."

"Bartenders and cabbies. We're the ones you tell your troubles to. Not these high-priced headshrinkers. All they want is your money."

"I hear that," muttered Jeannine.

"Idlewild," he announced. "As promised."

"That was quick. I expected it to be at least another thirty minutes. I . . . " her voice faded away as she looked out the window of the antique cab.

They had pulled up to an airport, but it wasn't the bustling, congested throng she was used to at Kennedy. No buses with liveries jockeying for position. No cement barriers. No crowds with matching luggage.

There was one building, a single runway, and a prop plane idling on the grass shy of the runway. On the tail, blue lettering spelled: Pan American Airlines.

"Pan Am?" said Jeannine. "Where the hell are we?"

She turned to the driver to scold him for obviously delivering her to some sort of antiques show, but this time she wasn't speaking to the back of a head or a rearview mirror. The cabbie, facing her now, had removed his sunglasses.

Words died in her throat.

The cabbie had no eyes.

"Idlewild, as promised," he said again. A too-wide smile slithered across his face.

"Who . . . what the fuck?" Jeannine had a sudden urge to pee as she held her briefcase close.

"Let this be a lesson to you, little *plaçage*," said the cabbie. "Take nothing at face value. Remember this. You will be in N'Orleans soon enough. The waters will speak to you, if you pay attention. The trees and the creatures will flatter you with lies. But hidden among those lies are whispers of truth. Listen to the whispers of the bayou, and you might just make it out alive."

The cabbie removed his hat, revealing two round wounds, one above each eye socket, filled with maggots.

"Take it from poor ole' Easy Street. I know."

The wipers slammed against the windscreen, the report of the blades akin to two gunshots, the water splashing off the windscreen like blood spraying from bullet holes.

Thump-shwa! Thump-shwa!

Jeannine threw herself back into the seat, eyes

wide, desperately trying to find the handle of the door, when a woman's voice said, "Miss, we're here. That's $27.50 and the credit card machine is broken."

Jeannine blinked once. Then twice.

She was in the back of a NYC cab—but not a classic car with a dead driver. It was a Prius, and a woman in a fleece with her hair pulled back in a bun was staring at her.

Horns blared, and a cop knocked on the windshield.

"Move it! You're blockin' the bus lane!"

"Please, miss. $27.50. And get out of my car. I don't want a crazy person in my cab no more!"

Jeannine grabbed a fifty from her wallet and handed it to the woman, who sped off without offering change as soon as Jeannine's carry-on was out of the car. Jeannine stood by the curb, shaking.

A vision. She'd had a vision. That hadn't happened since—since she'd left New Orleans over a decade ago.

"What the fuck is going on?" she asked.

The rain continued to fall, as throngs of people rolled luggage around her.

None of them answered her. None of them would even meet her eyes.

THREE

THE ROOM WAS sparse and smelled of old cigarettes and sweat. A worn table, chipped, with the word "fuck" scratched in its surface an impressive number of times, stood between the hand-cuffed man facing the two-way mirror and the man with his back to those watching and listening. A single dented lamp hung over the table, casting shadows along the walls and on the stained ceiling tiles. The room was supposed to intimidate. The room was supposed to scare those brought into it. For Curtis Jones, the room reminded him of his past.

He smiled at the thought.

The former cop had a dozen cuts and abrasions that had been hastily bandaged. The bump on his forehead throbbed, and he knew he'd have two black eyes by morning, but he had somehow miraculously survived.

Jones rubbed the tangled hair of his goatee. The old man with matted long hair that he watched in the mirror did the same. *When did I get so old?* He shifted in his seat—one of those cheap wooden chairs that was more uncomfortable than the pews at his church. A lit cigarette with an inch and a half of ash burned in the ashtray, just out of his reach. He looked longingly at the smoldering butt, then at his interrogator.

"You're in deep shit, Jonesy," said his old partner, Randy.

Curtis smiled even broader. This was a game he knew only too well.

"Brought you outta retirement for this, partner? How's Dolores? Send her my best, will you?" Curtis's voice sounded like gravel even to himself. No doubt due to his two-pack-a-day habit lubricated by bourbon.

"Don't fuck around," replied Randy. "This is serious. They found your old service revolver near those two skeletons—the gun you claimed went missing years back. Both skeletons had holes in the skulls indicative of what would be expected from a revolver. One bullet has already been retrieved and it's been matched to your missing gun."

"What a load of bullshit, and you know it." Curtis sat back in his chair, the cheap wood creaking under the strain. Narrowing his eyes at Randy, he asked, "Why you doing this? What're they giving you to interrogate me?"

"It's like this," said Randy, shifting in his own seat, his eyes not meeting Curtis's as he focused on picking an imaginary bit of dirt from under his fingernail. "I'm not your partner, Jonesy. You went over to the other side. I tried to help you after you left the force—"

"After I was fired, you mean," said Jones.

Randy slammed a hand down on the table. "We're not friends. Hell, I'm not even sure we ever were friends. Partners, sure. Maybe. Once. But that was a long time ago. Your rap sheet is as long as my arm now. And now they like you for a double murder. I never thought you'd go that far, man. But you were always a little weird when it came to that girl."

"You can play the "hurt partner" card all you want, Randy," said Jones, "but I know you as well as you know me. You *know* I'm being set up."

"Do I?" asked Randy, finally looking at Jones.

"You sure as hell do," snapped Curtis. "But the Major . . . he has you back working here when you should be fishing in the Gulf. Why?"

"Why did you commit murder?" said Randy, eyes blazing.

"You know I . . . " Curtis started to say when realization finally struck. "What's the Major got on you, boy?" asked Curtis.

Randy cleared his throat.

"Two men kidnapped Jeannine LaRue off the roof of her house right after Katrina. They took her, locked her in a cabin, and raped her for two months. You found her. You stayed with her in the hospital. You decked that TV psychologist asshole that exploited her story. It's not a stretch to think you tracked down and murdered the swamp rats that done took her. You always had a sweet spot for that girl, Curtis. You're also a fucking hothead. So, tell me what happened."

"Heh. You've got it all figured out, don'tcha?" Curtis leaned back in his chair.

"We have enough to empower a grand jury," replied Randy. "Save yourself some time. Save Jeannine the grief of reliving her experience to a packed courtroom. Help *her* to avoid all that media coverage."

"Fuck you, Randy," said Curtis. *This is what he*

wants. Stop. Think. Curtis's smile returned. "I know I'm being set up, man. Pretty sure you know it, too. So why are you helping the Major with this bullshit? You know he's as crooked as a three-dollar bill."

"He still has a badge," said Randy. "And a healthy hatred of you."

"'That don't mean shit in this parish and you know it, boss. Why are you-"

"Your gun," interrupted Randy, counting with his fingers. "Two dead bayou rats. Like I said, DA says it's enough, but I want to hear it from your mouth." Randy slapped the table, the sharp retort probably startling those behind the glass. But Curtis didn't move. Randy had been his partner for eight years—Curtis knew how the man worked.

Of course, Randy probably thought he knew how Curtis worked, too, but that was based on knowing Curtis before he took on his "retirement gig," back when he was on the right side of the law. Things were different now. He watched Randy's eyes flick back and forth, a bead of sweat rolling down one temple. *He's scared. What the fuck does the Major have on you, boy?*

"Don't suppose I could have a smoke, man?" asked Curtis. "If I fess up to you, it's gonna be a long story and we might be here a spell."

Randy picked up the nearly extinguished cigarette and slowly took a drag. Then he snuffed out the butt. "Tell me the story first, then I'll give ya the whole pack." Randy tossed a box of Marlboro Reds and a lighter—Curtis's Zippo—on the table, just out of the chained man's reach.

Smug fucker. He's in for a surprise. Curtis dropped his chained hands into his lap and leaned forward. "Remember when we were little? You used to come over to my house after school."

"So?" asked Randy, as he leaned back in his chair.

"Mama used to serve us hot treats. Crackers with melted cheese. We used to think we were so rich—a hot snack after school every day."

"I'll ask again: so?"

"Remember how disappointed we were to find out the snacks were old Triscuits way past their sell-by date with a sliver of government-issued cheese?"

"Yeah, I do." The ghost of a smile appeared on his face.

"Disappointment. We got used to it as kids. We expect it as adults. I hope they are paying you well for this, my man. If I was you, I'd ask for a bonus, though. And a big, fat retainer."

Randy sighed, amused. "Oh? Why is that?"

"Because they're gonna need you to find me when I break outta here. We'll split the retainer fifty-fifty. I'll even make the chase look convincing."

Randy laughed. "And that's attempted bribery added to the charges, you arrogant prick. You think you can get out of here? Just get up and walk out the door—a half-dozen cops are watching behind that glass." Randy aimed his thumb over his shoulder at the big wall mirror. "And another fifty uniforms on the floor. Even if you could get outta your chains, which you can't, you wouldn't get five feet before we all shot you dead."

He leaned in close enough for Curtis to smell his cigarette breath.

"There are a lotta boys who would love to put a bullet in you."

"They'll need to take a number," said Curtis,

blowing off Randy's jab. "Nah. I'm gonna go out the big hole that's about to appear in the south wall."

"Oh, really?" asked Randy. "You've gotten more delusional in your old age, partner. Besides, you're still chained to the damn table."

"Yeah. About that." Curtis lifted his now unchained hands to show Randy. He shrugged. "Army Ranger training. I recommended the department buy better restraints nearly twenty years ago. But do bureaucrats listen? No . . . "

Randy's eyes bulged. He opened his mouth to call for backup as he went for his personal gun, when the side wall of the interrogation room buckled with an ungodly crash, shattering the two-way mirror.

Distracted, Randy never saw the right cross that flattened him.

Cops screamed instructions at each other. Dust and curses flew. An alarm blared. As men and women picked themselves off the ground, they raised their hands slowly.

Curtis held Randy's revolver on them.

"I also mentioned moving the interrogation rooms away from the outside walls and building barricades between the parking lot and the building," said Curtis, addressing them all. "Guess that recommendation fell on deaf ears, too."

Out of the corner of his eye, Curtis caught movement as a young policewoman reached for her gun.

"Now, I'd hate to shoot a woman," he said, not looking directly at her. "But I will if you don't stop fussin'."

The policewoman froze in place.

"Jonesy," called a surly voice from the gaping maw

that had been the southern wall of the station. "You owe us a new truck."

"Yeah, yeah," muttered Curtis as he picked up the smokes and the lighter. "Get the rest of the krewe together and meet at the safe house. I'll be there shortly," he called to the faceless voice.

Shadows melted away from the destruction. Not far away, doors slammed and tires spun on pavement.

"I know how much you love your old guns," Jones said to Randy, who sat with the rest of the police officers, rubbing his jaw. "I'll get this back to you."

The Louisiana summer humidity rushed in through the new hole in the building, and Curtis began to sweat. The Major had one of those new Mercedes. Bet it had primo AC. And besides, Curtis needed a getaway car.

FOUR

AFTER THE CAB RIDE, Jeannine was barely able to make the Delta lounge before breaking down with a sob. A fellow flier took pity on her and bought her a martini. Jeannine should have said no, but she was shaking so hard all she could do was nod her head.

She should have said no to the next three martinis, as well.

Jeannine had been sober since college—no booze, no pills. She had to give it to Stanley. With his help she had learned to deal with the horrors of her past without self-medicating.

Stanley would be so disappointed in her right now. She felt that old familiar shame rising as bile in her throat.

She made the ladies room in time to empty the contents of her stomach. When her flight was called, she staggered out of the stall, only to have another woman look at her sideways and *tut* loudly.

Jeannine ignored her.

She washed her face, rinsed her mouth, and stumbled onto the concourse. She didn't remember

27

going through security, yet here she was fifty yards from her gate. She bought a pack of gum from the nearest Hudson News and made the last call for her flight to New Orleans.

The young white woman at the gate watched Jeannine's impaired approach. The attendant's body language said everything about her—uptight and judgmental, ready to tussle with a woman of color. How many times had she dealt with that attitude in the past? She'd lost count.

Jeannine was gearing herself for an argument when a black man wearing a Delta uniform, a nice smile, and sunglasses gently put his hand on the Delta bitch's shoulder, and then addressed Jeannine.

"Ah, Ms. LaRue," he said. "We were about to close the doors. Let me help you down the jetway."

Normally, she would have protested against an act of male bullshit chivalry. But she'd had way too much to drink. *I'm really fucking drunk.* Instead of protesting, she gratefully let the man take her by the elbow. He helped her to her first-class seat.

"Thank you," she slurred to the man.

"Glad to help, ma'am. That's what I'm here for, you dig?"

He gave her another big, bright smile after strapping her in and left the cabin, whistling a blues riff.

Why is he so familiar? Damn booze . . . can't think . . .

Jeannine fell asleep in the middle of the flight attendants' safety lecture.

⚜

The miniature ghost stood defiant, hands on hips, with a fire in the deep brown eyes peering through the sheet holes that would have given most larger beings pause. But where the frayed sheet ended, a pair of long, gangly legs wearing pink "Hello Kitty" socks and blue thrift-shop sneakers comically softened the spirit's fierce glare.

"I wore this at Halloween when I was, like, ten," sulked the irate specter.

An elderly black woman with close-cropped curly white hair sighed in response as she looked down at her adopted granddaughter. "Jeannine LaRue, you're the one who begged me to have a costume party for your birthday in the middle of summer, Lord have mercy."

"Nana! I'm fourteen now, and the sheet don't—"

"Not for another two days you ain't, young lady. Dinner is nearly ready; go wash your hands." Nana shook her head, a smile twitching on her lips. "And set the table, Mademoiselle Fantôme. As the young specter sped toward the washroom, Nana called. "I'll tell you another Voodoo story about your ma, if you're good!"

"Cassandra!" shouted the costumed Jeannine, sheet billowing behind her as she headed toward the tiniest bedroom. "Nana wants us to set the table! And we're getting a story!"

Jeannine side-eyed her Nana, as a flicker of disapproval crossed the elder LaRue's face. The teen tried not to smile at her little rebellious verbal victory. Mama. Cassandra. We were all the same anyway, she thought.

Nana frowned after her grandniece. Most of her neighborhood had rejected Jeannine—her skin wasn't dark enough to fit in. The few friends the little girl did have were mixed-race like she was. How is *it that people could be so cruel to a young girl? But the world was cruel, the elder LaRue well understood having grown up in a segregated South.*

Heavy wind battered the small row home, rattling windows and pulling Nana out of her own thoughts. She was used to storms—this was N'Orleans after all. She stepped to the simmering pot of gumbo, sniffing critically at the air. Dipping a spoon into the sauce, she confirmed what her nose already told her. "Definitely more hot sauce," she muttered. She crossed to the kitchen window and picked up a large bottle.

The wind rattled the window again, harder this time. Nana's smile turned to a frown.

From the living room TV, the voice of a panicked weatherman pleaded with the local viewers to evacuate. Then, the picture turned to static. A dark silence replaced the hiss as the power failed completely.-

Nana had never evacuated before. She wasn't going to leave her home now.

That was her last mistake.

The living room window surrendered first. The frame squealed in protest, then ripped from the wall. Jeannine and another figure ran into the room toward Nana. Glass shattered around their heads as the frame roared away into the black abyss. Jeannine screamed but the sound was drowned out by the wind that turned candlesticks into missiles, utensils into shrapnel.

With the home open to the elements, Nana grabbed Jeannine, and she in turn grabbed her mother's small hand.

Cassandra was in her Mardi Gras outfit, with

white skeleton makeup on her black skin, wearing a karabela dress of cobalt blue. Little animal bones tied together with a bit of leather hung from her neck.

But . . . she was small, not tall like Nana. Why was Mamma so small? young Jeannine thought.

Nana's hand was sweaty. She was nervous, Jeannine knew. The wringing hands always gave her away. But she had Nana and her mother, so there was nothing to fear. They would all be okay.

The wind howled louder, and the rain lashed horizontally. White resin chairs flew in through the rectangular hole in the wall and bounced off the walls, shattering the remaining pictures. But the cacophony of the raging storm was gradually supplanted by another sound—growing louder as the seconds ticked by.

Rushing water poured down the street.

Death was coming. Riding those waves like a jockey of the damned, while the pungent smell of sulfur and brimstone mixed with the musty scent of damp earth and sewage.

"Hurry," Nana called to the two sets of wide brown eyes looking up at her. "We need to get up to the attic."

A wall of water, froth, and debris blasted through the street, slamming into Nana's house, wrenching it partially off its foundation. The damaged building groaned once but stayed in place. The brackish water mercilessly assaulted the walls and doors. Jeannine stood at the top of the attic ladder, her mother right below her, when a section of the east wall splintered and disappeared into the inky blackness of the rising flood. Farther down the ladder, the frigid, shit-smelling water was up to

Nana's waist as she tried to climb. Jeannine watched in detached horror as her little mother slipped on the steps, mouth opening wide. Cassandra must have been screaming, but Jeannine couldn't hear over the tempest raging around them.

Her mother fell, pulling Nana off the ladder as she did, and both slipped under the tar-like froth as the rest of the east wall of the house was reduced to kindling.

Nana and Mamma were gone.

Jeannine screamed as the waters swirled higher, hungry for another soul. She kept climbing the ladder and, from overhead, Jeannine heard what sounded like teeth gnashing at the roof. With a final tearing sound, the plaster sloughed off from the ceiling while cascading wooden rafters tried to knock her into the rising pool below. Rain pelted Jeannine and her blood streamed from a dozen cuts as a hole appeared in the roof above, beckoning to her. The waters below reached higher and higher. Above, the wind shrieked, redoubling its triumphant calling for her blood.

Jeannine scrambled through the jagged hole in the roof, climbing into the mouth of Satan himself, as torrents of rain and wind begged her to join Nana and Cassandra. Slipping, Jeannine sliced her calf on a splintered rafter, the gaping wound spurting blood into a storm that was eager for it. But Jeannine wasn't ready for death. She held onto her shattered home, finding purchase on some exposed timbers, fingers and palms bleeding with the effort to hold on.

As she lay there, gasping for breath, a pair of black feet appeared on the same beam she clung to.

Looking up, she saw the feet belonged to her mother, Cassandra, now towering above her daughter.

Something about Cassandra's appearance terrified Jeannine.

"Where's Nana?" screamed Jeannine.

Cassandra stood stock-still, her balance somehow unaffected by the lashing wind and rain. Her hair hung over her eyes in a curtain of matted tangles and filth. She pulled back the limp strands and looked at Jeannine. Her face was still covered by a painted candy skull—but the paint was running down her face: white tears melting into the storm.

Cassandra's eyes were now ice blue, illuminated with some inner light.

She held out her hand to her daughter, laughing.

"No!" shouted Jeannine, recoiling. "Leave me alone!"

"Take my hand," said Cassandra. "I'll save you."

Cassandra smiled, showing pointed teeth. Black sludge oozed from her mouth.

"I told you before, no!" Jeannine screamed again, and her mother, standing above her, was still neither moved by the wind, by the rain, by Jeannine's tears.

"Suit yourself, child."

In an instant, Cassandra was gone.

FIVE

Greenwood Cemetery Caretaker's Cottage
New Orleans

T HE "SAFE PLACE" was a cemetery.
       One of the krewe—Richard "Red Rooster"
Romain, a black Baptist with a penchant for the
occult—worked as the caretaker and lived in the small
cottage nestled between the stone and marble above-
ground graves.

"The neighbors don't put up much of a fuss," he'd
once said when asked why he liked living surrounded
by the dead. But Jones knew the truth had to do more
with the former Ranger's interest in Voodoo, than it
did with peace and quiet.

A three-legged cat let out a loud "meow" as Curtis
entered the dimly lit cottage. The place smelled of
fried sausage and peppers, and the growl from his
stomach reminded him the last time he'd had
something to eat was a cold slice of pizza earlier that
day.

"Rooster!" Jones called. "Hey, Roo!" He
deliberately made a lot of noise as the old man of his
krewe had a blown eardrum from the war. Probably
only one of a handful of soldiers whose Purple Heart
was due to an exploding still.

The cat rubbed against Jones's leg, purring madly.

"'llo Ollie. Where's your papa, hmm?" he asked, as he bent down to scratch the old cat behind the ears.

A voice called from the kitchen, "Jonesy, that better be you playing with my cat, or I'm gonna fill your ass with buckshot."

"Jesus H. Christ, Roo," yelled Curtis. "You blind as well as deaf?"

"Don't you blaspheme in *my* house, Curtis Jones!"

"Sorry," muttered Jones. Louder, he asked, "Where's the rest of the krewe?"

"They'll be along," said Roo.

Jones walked into the kitchen in time to catch Rooster setting down the shotgun he had leveled at Jones and picking up a wooden spoon.

"The boys had to throw the cops off their trail after they rammed our stolen armored truck into police HQ, didn't they?" asked Rooster as he stood at the stove.

Rooster's back was to him, but Jones could see the tension in the old man's shoulders. He walked up next to Rooster and said, changing the subject, "Smells good."

Rooster grunted. "Not ready yet. I used some of them green peppers you like from New Mexico. Sauce tastes all right, but there isn't no kick." He glanced furtively at Jones.

"Okay, Roo," said Jones, knowing what was coming. "Spit it out."

Romain turned, pointing the spoon at him. "We planned that heist for near-on a year. Hell, it took six months to steal and restore that old, armored truck. And, tonight, because you wanted to go zippin' around in your hot rod, we gave away our truck to the damn cops."

35

Jones scowled. "Okay, I get you're pissed. But this is bigger than any heist. You know as well as I do that som'in unnatural is happening. It's been building since Katrina."

"Is that why you threw away six months of planning?" grumbled Roo. "Because 'som'in unnatural is happening' or is it because of the girl?"

Curtis felt his face grow hot and looked away. "Jeannine has nothing to do with this. The Biloxi and Miami people. Nightmare. The Major. We were too small time for them. Nobody would have expected us to pull off something like this. They would have been pointing fingers at one another for years. But there is something bigger going on, Roo. Trust me on that. That's why I had you guys torch my place . . . I—"

"I'm hearin' a lot of 'I' this and 'I' that. But *we* were working on this score. Together," said Roo. "This heist would have set us all up for life. We ain't getting any younger, Jonesy. You think Gallow wants to run that restaurant for the rest of his life? No. He wants to be governor someday. You need money to do that. What about Lil' Dave? He wants to retire to a villa in Puerto Rico surrounded by his grandbabies."

"And what do you and the Golem want?" asked Jonesy.

Roo's shoulders sagged. "I like the life we had, man. Running little scams, makin' some money. The adventures got the blood flowing. I ain't got no family, just us. I liked that we had some fun that bothered no one."

"I thought you said we were getting old?"

"True. But what we were doin' wasn't really hurting no one. It was the perfect retirement gig. But then you go and get the rest of the boys all excited about that armored truck deal. And maybe me, too. Why?"

"There is something bigger going on and I wanted a piece of the action," said Curtis.

"Bullshit," grunted Romain, and turned back to his sausage and peppers. "'Som'in unnatural is happening' my ass. Thought you didn't believe in all the mumbo-jumbo."

"Goddamn it, you're the one who clued *us* into the weird shit! Now you're ignoring—"

Clank!

The iron skillet fell to the floor, splattering its contents every which way.

"Now, you listen, and you listen good, Curtis Jones. You've made fun of me and my beliefs since the war. Why would you give a shit about the "weirdness," as you call it, *now*, right before the score that would set us all up for the rest of our lives? *It was your idea in the first place!*"

Jones and Rooster were practically standing toe to toe. The 5'9" Rooster looked up at the 6'3" Jones, fire in his eyes. Jones ground his teeth.

"It wasn't my idea," said Jones. "And because, you were right all along, and I was wrong. And I didn't wanna fuckin' believe it, is all."

"Oh. Just like that. You didn't wanna believe it. What are you, a goddamn child? The world *is*. It ain't what we want it to be, you dumb—"

"I saw Cassandra."

"—honky . . . What?"

"Jeannine's mother. She came to me six months ago."

"That's not possible."

"Not possible," snorted Curtis. "When Charley took a mortar round, who brought him back?"

"That's different. And if you remember, you didn't believe me when I told you what I'd done."

37

"I was out for the count. The boys told me you worked a miracle that day. And I didn't believe them or you. But that was then."

"Cassandra don't exist no more. You know that."

"Aren't you the one always trying to convince me there is more to this world than we've been told? Five minutes after I dreamed about her coming to see me, Jeannine called for the first time in years. Said she was gonna take the Louisiana bar, not the New York one, because *Cassandra* told her to. And six months later, the cops want me for a double murder I didn't do."

"What the hell is going on in here?" shouted a third voice. It was the Golem, also known as Charley Mouton. Mouton was of average height, clean-shaven, with white, curly hair and Coke-bottle glasses. The lines in his white skin made him appear older than he was. He hobbled in, leaning heavily on his cane, eyes darting back and forth between Jones and Romain. Behind him were Li'l Dave Fernández—a 5'3" man of Puerto Rican descent, who always had a wad of chewing tobacco in his cheek—and Carl Gallow, the impeccably groomed and dressed restaurateur who was, to hear him tell, a direct descendent of the original French settlers of the region. All the men were former Army Rangers: friends and brothers in a way only military men who served together in wartime understood.

All of them were now criminals.

The whole krewe was here.

Jones relaxed his clenched fists and let his shoulders slump. "We'll finish this later," he said, and bent to pick up the fallen skillet.

"Leave it," said Rooster. "I'll order a bunch o' po' boys for everyone."

"Fine," said Jones, his anger still threatening to boil over.

"What the hell, Jonesy?" asked Mouton again.

"Thanks for getting me out of that place, Golem," replied Jones, ignoring the question.

"Sure," replied Mouton. "But what're you two fighting about and why is there sausage and peppers all over the floor?"

"Well, I . . . wait." Jones looked around the room. "Guys, where is Jeannine? I thought you were gonna get her at the airport while I led the cops away from my place?"

"It's like this, Jonesy," said Carl in his soft baritone. "My connections told me that your place was too hot, so we had to wait for a while before we could get into your double-wide to clear it. Golem and I barely got back in time to bust you out of the sheriff's building."

"We never had time to go to the airport," piped in Fernández.

"So, she's back and no one was at the airport to get her?" said Jones, exasperated that he was already letting Jeannine down. He looked at his watch. "If we hurry, we might catch her, figuring a wait for her bag."

"Is that wise, Curtis?" asked Carl. "You just broke out of jail. The police will be looking everywhere for you. My manager called and told me they searched my restaurant."

"I'm feeling lucky tonight," said Curtis, as he headed for the front door.

"Take a moment to breathe, for Chrissake!" said Gallow, worry in his voice. "You were in a fucking major car accident a couple hours ago!"

Curtis stared at Gallow until the man looked away.

"I feel awesome, thanks for asking. Better than I've felt in years," said Curtis to the room. "Now, Roo, get your big-ass truck goin'. We're doin' an airport run."

SIX

Louis Armstrong International Airport
New Orleans

AN ASIAN-LOOKING flight attendant—
a woman too young to be working
full-time, in Jeannine's opinion—sat with
the shaken attorney as the rest of the passengers
disembarked.

"It was only a nightmare," she told the young
attendant. "Too many drinks before getting on board.
I'll be fine in a minute. Honestly, you don't have to
stay with me."

"It's not a problem," said the Delta cheerleader
with a toothy smile. "Gets me out of picking up other
people's booger rags stuffed in the seat cushions."

Jeannine's stomach lurched. "Nice," was all she
could say without grabbing an airsick bag.

The last passenger—an old man with a cane—
finally exited the aircraft.

"I'm okay," said Jeannine to the attendant.
"Really. I can just go grab my bag and get a cab to my
hotel—"

"Jeannine LaRue?"

A short man with a buzz cut appeared. He wore a
cheap suit under a damp trench coat and stood

flanked by two uniformed cops. The three of them blocked the aisle.

"Who is asking?" replied Jeannine as she collected her belongings.

"I'm Major Thomas Dufresne of the St. Dismas Sheriff's Office, ma'am," replied the buzz-cut man. "I was wondering if you had a few minutes to talk with us."

The Major? Fuck. Hold it together, girl.

"You are a little out of your jurisdiction, Major, aren't you?"

The man smiled. It was a plastic smile that never reached his eyes. Jeannine got the sense he'd practiced in front of a mirror.

"Yes, ma'am. However, we would like a quick word. I'm happy to wait for a warrant and a state trooper, if you wish."

Jeannine looked at the attendant, who now wouldn't meet her gaze. The niceness had been a ruse to keep her here until the cops arrived.

Damn. I should've known. No more drinking, Ice Queen!

"Your job is done, sweetie. Go clean the beer farts from the seats, 'kay?" Turning to the Major, she added, "Let's wait on the staties, shall we? Or better yet, let's call the Orleans Parish District Attorney. I have her number in my phone . . . "

"Ms. LaRue," said the Major, that fake smile never leaving his face. "I'm here as a courtesy. There was an accident this evening and I have some bad news for you. I wanted to take you someplace quiet to tell you, as I heard you were . . . unwell on this flight."

Jeannine's heart leapt into her throat. *Curtis . . .*

"Why don't you tell me what's happened, Major?"

She hoped the words had come out stronger than she felt.

"As you wish," replied the Major. He reached into the pocket of his trench coat and pulled out a small notebook. "You knew a Curtis Jones, yes?"

"Knew?"

"Yes, I'm afraid there was an accident this evening. Apparently, he was driving—according to my deputies—at a high rate of speed and lost control of his car."

Oh, God. Curtis.

"I'm afraid he was killed on impact, ma'am. I'm so sorry."

No, you're not.

The Major closed his notebook and put it away. "He was on his way to pick you up, I'm guessing. I understand you are . . . were . . . his attorney, correct?"

The shock of Curtis's death sobered Jeannine almost immediately—at least enough to think clearly. *The Major must know what Curtis thinks . . . thought of him. He must also presume I've been told of his mistrust toward this man. So, what game was he playing?*

"Yes, I . . . am Curtis's lawyer."

How could this happen now? When they'd actually started to mend their relationship after a decade of near silence and . . . no! Don't think that. Not now. Stay focused, girl.

"His old police partner has already identified the body, Ms. LaRue. But we need to clear up a few things, and I'm hoping you'll come with us to finalize paperwork, et cetera. I know this isn't why you came down here, but Curtis *was* a cop for me for a long time. I'd like to see things done respectfully."

His words were right, but Jeannine thought both the Major's tone and body language were off.

"Major, this is . . . " Jeannine was leery. While that last sentence sounded sincere, cops were good liars—they were trained to be. And crooked cops *had* to be to stay out of prison as long as the Major had. She took a deep breath.

"Major, I want to thank you for coming here to meet me in person to tell me this." Lawyers were taught to lie, too. "If I could collect my things and have the evening to recover from being both sick and in shock from this news, I would very much appreciate it."

The Major looked at her, eyes narrowed, searching.

Jeannine continued, "I would be happy to meet you at your parish office first thing in the morning."

Laughter came from the back of the plane. The Major's head jerked up.

Jeannine turned to see the flight crew working the aisle, then looked back toward the Major.

That's right, you bastard. Too many witnesses around for you to pull anything.

The Major stared at her; his eyes unblinking.

"That would, of course, be acceptable, Ms. LaRue," he said finally. "I'm terribly sorry for your loss. Here is my business card. Please, feel free to call me in the morning and I will make arrangements to have you brought to my office."

The Major turned to his two henchmen. "Let's go, boys."

Jeannine watched the three men leave the plane, then took her time gathering her briefcase and checking her seat for "any personal items" before slowly exiting to the jetway.

BAYOU WHISPERS

The sticky humidity that surrounded her was something familiar, yet foreboding—a reminder she had returned to the place her family died and where she . . .

She . . .

No. Don't think of it. You can't fall apart now. There are things at play and Curtis would never . . .

She stopped, placing a hand on the Delta kiosk at the gate. A sob threatened to burst out of her chest. Stanley, for all his faults, had taught her how to deal with these runaway thoughts. The anxiety. She closed her eyes for a moment and steadied her breathing.

Curtis would never want to see you break down like this. Focus, Ice Queen. Focus.

She opened her eyes. The weight on her chest was gone. Throngs of sweaty people passed her by as the airport air conditioning tried to keep the infamous New Orleans humidity at bay.

Bags. Hotel. Then calls. I need to find Curtis's krewe and figure out what's really going on. There is no way the Major was here just to give me the bad news in person. Was anything that prick said true? Oh my God . . . Curtis . . .

"Ma'am, are you okay?" A Delta agent approached her to help.

Jeannine waved away the agent. She checked the signs and walked toward baggage claim.

The krewe had watched the Major from the dual cab of Rooster's F-350 pickup. The little boss and his two goons had come out of the airport terminal and gotten into an unmarked car. The officers held the back door open for the Major like they were preprogrammed server drones.

Which, Jones thought, they pretty much were.

He remembered his own academy training only too well.

Ten minutes later, Jeannine appeared, and Jones's heart skipped a beat. She was an adult now—of course, he knew that she was twenty-six. But her hair was the same kinky mess it had been the first night he'd seen her. *This must be how a divorced parent feels when they haven't seen their kids in a while.* He hadn't expected so much change in her appearance. His one regret in life was that he never got to be a parent—a flesh and blood father or an adoptive one, it wouldn't have mattered. Seeing her now, he realized how much of her life he'd missed—all due to stupidity on both their parts.

Not that he'd ever admit his guilt and regret to anyone.

Jeannine was looking down at her phone—something was wrong. Jones could see it in her face.

"Oh, she don't look happy," said Roo, as if he'd been reading Jones's mind.

"Nope," was all Curtis replied. What he *wanted* to say was, "I'll be back in a minute," and then go hug the woman who was as close to a daughter as he'd ever had.

But he wouldn't do that. Especially not with the Major and his boys watching her from a hundred yards away.

Besides, she'd probably belt him.

Jones watched as Jeannine let out a long breath and practically stomped her foot on the ground. *What had pissed her off now?* His thought was interrupted when an Escalade pulled up to the curb right in front of her.

BAYOU WHISPERS

Jeannine stood outside the airport with her bag, waiting on the Uber she'd ordered. The first driver the app selected dropped her immediately. The second driver dropped her, too.

"Motherfucker," swore Jeannine. She'd never seen two drivers drop her like that. It was weird for a service that had always been reliable. Sure, some New York City taxis wouldn't stop for her, but the Uber drivers didn't even know what she looked like. She was about to walk to the taxi stand when a big black Escalade pulled up, beeping its horn.

Jeannine didn't move toward the vehicle. The last time she'd gotten into a vehicle she wasn't expecting— her memory of that maggot-eyed cabbie was too fresh.

The back door of the Escalade opened. A heavy-set, middle-aged man emerged. From the other side of the vehicle, a woman got out. She held a video camera.

"Need a lift?" said the man with a smile.

"I should've known you wouldn't leave me alone, Stanley," said Jeannine.

❧

Before Jeannine's cab ride with Easy Street

"Sorry I'm late, Stanley. This rain is awful."

The speaker was a tall woman—nearly six feet in flats. Jeannine LaRue held herself with confidence and professionalism. The outside world would never guess at the seething vat of emotions and pain she kept locked away. Only her blue eyes gave any hint. They were always searching, calculating. Life was a chess game to Jeannine, and she had become a grand master.

"The rain in Brooklyn Heights always smells weird," she said, as she placed her wet umbrella in the stand. "They say rain cleans a city, renews it. But all I smell is water, concrete, and desperation. Why is that, do you think?"

The office of Doctor Stanley Bernstein, PhD was in a posh old section of Brooklyn that now commanded more rent money than some of the flashiest Manhattan high-rises. The suite of rooms was furnished in dark woods polished to a fine sheen, which left the entire brownstone smelling lemony fresh.

"I don't know," said Stanley Bernstein. "Why do you think that is?"

Jeannine snorted.

"It's not a problem—you being late," said the balding, middle-aged man sitting on one of the dark leather waiting room couches. It was probably polished with Pledge, as well.

"Of course it's not a problem for you, Stanley. You bill out at $350 an hour."

The man looked over his trifocals at Jeannine and smiled. "True. And it's nice to get paid a tidy sum to read *People*." He tossed the magazine on the coffee table—not *People*, but the latest issue of *Psychology Today*. She looked at the professional trade mag, then back at her therapist. He stared at her intently.

"We going to do this in your lobby, or can we go into your equally dark office with the holy shrine to your daytime Emmy?"

"Yes. My first nationally televised show. Thank you for that."

"Glad my pain was useful for your television career."

The man said nothing as he rose, leading the way down a thick-pile crimson-carpeted hallway, past a water feature that burbled away merrily. Jeannine followed, only the barest hint of a limp.

Normal people were probably impressed with the opulence of the cherub-encrusted fountain. It only made Jeannine remember she hadn't peed before she left her apartment.

Stanley's office continued the dark, drab motif of the lobby. It reminded her of an old, stuffy gentlemen's club where politics of the world and the subjugation of women were discussed in a haze of cigar smoke. The leather chairs and sofa were overstuffed and comfortable, though. She tossed her wet trench coat over the arm of the chair Stanley normally sat in during a session. She watched his face twitch once in recognition of her small power play.

He took the couch.

"So, I assume you heard the news?" he asked.

"Why did you lie to me?"

"Excuse me?"

"Stanley, please don't bullshit me. Just then, in your lobby, why did you lie to me?"

"About the magazine?"

"Yeah."

"Why do you think I did?"

"Oh, for fuck's sake, Stanley!" Jeannine stood and began to pace the office. The desk stood in one corner of the room, allowing for pacing. Stanley had moved it after Jeannine's first session, when she had

49

mentioned that sometimes she liked to pace while talking. She should be nicer to him, really. She just didn't feel like it.

"I think you lied to me because fucking with people is your hobby. Some people work on cars or play computer games. You fuck with people. You like them off balance and jittery."

"Yes, that's all true. But that's not why I did it."

Jeannine stopped and turned to the older man. "Then why?"

Stanley shook his head and reached over to the table next to the couch, where he picked up a thick folder wrapped with multiple rubber bands. "You're an attorney and you can't figure out why I told you a simple and obvious lie?"

Jeannine went back to pacing. She felt Stanley's eyes on her as she walked to where his Emmy was displayed.

"Do you mind if I ask you a legal question?" he asked.

"Oh dear. Are you in some sort of *legal* trouble for lying, Stanley?" mocked Jeannine.

Stanley ignored Jeannine's tone and continued, "My question is regarding *stare decisis*—that's when a judge is bound by precedent, yes?"

She stopped pacing and met Stanley's eyes.

"Sure," she said slowly, "but most judges base their decisions on their own interpretation of the law. Why?"

"And *jurisprudence constante* is when multiple cases are used as persuasive arguments for a new decision?"

"Well, sure, but that's secondary," she said automatically. "When—shit." Jeannine looked away from Stanley and began pacing once more. Stanley smiled.

"So, back in the spring, when you told me that you were sitting for the bar exam—"

"I didn't lie about that!" Jeannine broke in.

"No, you didn't. You did sit for a bar exam. My producers checked. But when we were looking into it, we discovered, much to *my* chagrin, that the New York bar, which is what you *told* me you were sitting for, happens to be on the same day as the *Louisiana* bar. And what I just asked you . . ."

"Okay. You caught me. Louisiana laws are different than the rest of the states. Very clever."

"Based, as they are, on French laws as opposed to British law."

"Actually, they are based on French, Spanish, and Roman—"

"Don't deflect, Jeannine."

"Fuck off, Stanley. So, I lied to you about which exam I was sitting. So what? It's my life."

"I've been trying for years to help you to fit in here. I walk in powerful circles and the people I know in New York could make your career for you."

"Stanley, these powerful people you talk about all look down on me when you aren't in the room. They respect you. They don't respect me."

"So, it's the race thing again."

"Stanley, of *course* it's a race thing." Jeannine's nostrils flared, and her ice-blue eyes blazed in anger. "It's a race thing, a woman in a man's world thing, it's a person with a disability thing. I check all the 'undesirable' boxes, as far as your powerful friends are concerned. I'll *never* be the blonde, white bombshell with the balls of brass that play in your power-tie-wearing, elite, misogynistic circle."

Stanley met her furious gaze with a calm, detached, unblinking stare of his own. He sighed.

"Okay, today we have stubborn and obstreperous Jeannine. I understand that, of course, based on today's news."

"What news?"

Stanley opened the folder and took a newspaper clipping off the top. The newsprint was crisp, the paper still white. It was from the morning's *Times*. Jeannine reached for it, but Stanley stopped her.

"Let me tell you about it first, then you can read it. Fair enough?"

"Sure."

"Dateline St. Dismas Parish, Louisiana. Disgraced former detective Curtis Jones of 5562A Crescent Road was arrested in the early morning hours under suspicion of murder. Two bodies . . . "

Jeannine started to pace again, and Stanley folded up the story.

"Ah. You've read it. Another lie."

"So?"

"Jeannine. It's been twelve years since that horror. This is going to bring it all back into the spotlight."

"I'll ask you again. So?"

"Jeannine!"

"Stanley, I've been in therapy for over a decade. And I have, as you so nicely stated, gone on to do some pretty intense stuff with my life. Yes, I still have the nightmares. Yes, I still have issues with men—although I'll remind you that my last boyfriend was—"

"Your last one-night stand, you mean."

"—was white, I was going to say. And it lasted a

week and a half, fuck you very much. *And* we had a lot of sex."

"Sex was never your issue, Jeannine. Personal connections are. Relationships are."

"Can I help it if most people suck? What is this really about, Stanley?"

"I want to walk through what you're feeling, here."

"I'm pissed. Curtis never killed anyone."

"Oh? And how do you know that?"

"I can read a legal brief, Stanley."

"Mmmm. Let me ask you a question. Why did you want to meet today? Your next appointment is Friday."

"As I told your secretary yesterday, I have a thing on Friday and didn't want to miss an appointment. She said you had time today and here I am."

"Yesterday. Interesting."

"I fucking hate it when you do that, Stanley."

The corners of the therapist's mouth twitched. "I find it interesting that you called before the *Times* article hit the newsstand. So now we're back to why I lied to you about the magazine I was reading."

"I . . . what?"

Stanley sighed. "Why did I lie to *you*?"

"Because you are a control freak who is living his twisted version of Foucault's world of sexual power?"

"Deflect all you want, but you needed to see that lies can be found out. The simple ones. The darker ones. The ones buried so deep you think no one will dig deep enough to find them. Eventually, the truth is uncovered."

"Tell that to Jimmy Hoffa."

"I need you to tell me what's going on. You told me you were sitting for the New York bar exam, yet you sat for the Louisiana bar instead. That's a completely different set of laws to study. You've been planning to go back to Louisiana for a while now."

"I miss turtle soup."

"Jeannine . . . "

"And walking around the French Quarter with a boozy hurricane . . . "

"Jeannine!"

"Stanley, I need to go back. I need to face it . . . and to face him. Curtis needs me."

Stanley stood. He rarely became angry, but the few times Jeannine had seen him upset, red blotches appeared on his face. They now crawled up from his neckline clear to his earlobes.

"If you go back, even a decade later, you might not be able to process the experience. Your psyche could completely collapse, causing permanent psychological damage. Look," said Stanley, a bead of sweat appearing at his brow line, "returning to where you were brutally held hostage—the sort of trauma you experienced, the loss of your leg . . . distance has helped the healing, to be sure. But you're not ready to go back there. Not yet. Do you get that?"

"I'm as ready as I need to be."

"What does that even mean? You are one of the brightest people I've ever met. IQ in the 140s, Exposition cognition off the charts."

Jeannine stopped pacing again, her back now turned toward her therapist.

"I have to go," she whispered.

"Why in God's name do you *have* to?"

"It's Curtis. He's the only one I trusted for a very long time. He's the only one who was there at the end of . . . "

"He saved you."

"Yeah."

"And now you are going to save him. Do you think he's forgiven you for leaving the way you did?"

Jeannine turned to look at Stanley. She was furious, but not at him. She'd shown her hand before she was ready, which meant Stanley would smell another opportunity for an Emmy. Time to change tact.

"Stanley. I lost my *leg*, Goddamn it. And that wasn't the worst of it, as you well know. I was so lost, but Curtis found and saved me."

Jeannine looked down at Stanley. He looked unflinchingly back up to her. The silence between them was as thick and heavy as a swamp. Or a Louisiana summer's day.

"Yes, I'm going to save him," she finally answered.

"Why?"

"Two reasons. First, he called and hired me after they arrested him. I'm his lawyer, and I'm sure he didn't do it." She picked up her trench coat from the arm of the chair and made her way to the door, swooping up the umbrella as she passed the stand.

"What's the second?"

"I owe him. I don't like having a debt hanging above my head. Conversation over."

"What about all I've done for you? What about your debt to *me*?"

The door slammed behind her and Stanley's Emmy fell off the mantle. He picked it off the thick carpet and set it back in its proper spot, giving the award a loving caress with his thumb in the process.

"Damn," Stanley muttered to the empty office. "I hate being right."

The rain outside fell harder as he picked up his mobile and called his producer.

"Karen, it's Stanley. She's going, it's confirmed. Have the TV crew meet me at LaGuardia in ninety minutes and call my driver."

Louis Armstrong International Airport

While Curtis and his krewe couldn't see who got out nearest to Jeannine, they did see the woman with the large professional-looking video camera resting on her shoulder quickly make her way around the back of the massive SUV.

"Oh, fuck no," said Jones, and reached for the door handle. Roo was seated farthest from Jones and couldn't help hold him. But Gallow and Charley grabbed him and got the door closed.

Curtis pushed his krewe off him.

"Jonesy, stop struggling!" shouted Roo. "We gotta wait and see what happens . . . "

The woman with the camera got back into the Escalade. A moment later, a middle-aged man put a suitcase in the back of the truck. He got into the vehicle and then it pulled away from the curb.

"Follow that som'bitch!" snarled Jones.

"Wait," said Gallow. "Look."

An unmarked police SUV pulled out after the Escalade. It must be the Major's goon squad.

"Now we go," said Gallow, tapping Roo's seat. "Roo, stay close, but not too close. Got it?"

BAYOU WHISPERS

The big Ford rumbled after the Major and Jeannine. Roo's truck fell in behind both the Escalade and the Major's car.

Jones finally shrugged Charley's grip off of him.

"I'm fine. Let go of me," he said. "Let's see where the som'bitch Stanley Bernstein is taking her,"

SEVEN

February 2006
WGNO Temporary Studio Outside the Louisiana
Superdome

"**D**ON'T BE NERVOUS," said Stanley with a reassuring smile. "You've done TV before. I'll be with you the whole time. Look at me if you get nervous, okay?"

"I'll be fine, Uncle Stanley," said fourteen-year-old Jeannine. "You worry too much."

"The people want an update on you," continued Stanley as if she hadn't spoken. "Talk about your new prosthetic. And don't forget to mention the charity event next week. That will lead right into the announcement of my new talk show."

"I know, Uncle Stanley!"

"And don't call me "uncle" on the air, okay? Might give people the wrong impression, got it?"

Jeannine nodded.

"Say you've got it."

She sighed. "I've got it, *Stanley.*"

"That's my girl," he said, as he put his arm around her shoulders.

"One minute, Dr. Bernstein," said the news director.

BAYOU WHISPERS

❧

Back in the make-shift green room, Curtis Jones, in his dress uniform, paced nervously while watching the broadcast. He'd be called when it was his turn to be interviewed. But it wasn't only the TV cameras that were making Curtis nervous. In the glovebox of his patrol car was the final paperwork to adopt Jeannine.

Before he'd met this incredible teenager, he'd been ambivalent at best regarding children. Spending time with Jeannine—what an amazingly strong person she was. Curtis wanted to teach her about the real world. Protect her from the predators until she could protect herself. True, she had emotional and physical scars. Didn't everyone? But somehow, Jeannine had persevered.

Besides, Georgina had insisted they try, once she knew who Jeannine was and what she'd been through.

Curtis thought of her as a daughter. His partner, Randy, who had four kids of his own, wouldn't let up on the teasing. "Papa Jonesy," he'd called him.

Georgina had called him the same thing.

He smiled at the thought.

"Ninety seconds, Officer Jones," said a young-looking man with a headset, scribbling madly on a clipboard. Curtis nodded.

He hated this publicity nonsense. Hated the fact this therapist guy had whisked Jeannine away from her rehab center in Baton Rouge to do a morning show. Jeannine had watched an interview with this smooth-talking, intelligent doctor while in her hospital room and liked what she saw.

Stanley Bernstein gave Jones the creeps.

But the opportunity to be on the local news show had helped Jeannine shake her fear and depression. Since the first meeting where she stammered her praise for the man, Jeannine had redoubled her efforts in rehab. She had stopped having the nightmares that plagued her every time she closed her eyes. She'd even stopped crying when talking about her Nana and Cassandra, which Jones found somewhat unsettling.

"We're nearing the top of the hour," said the cheery male newscaster on the TV monitor. "But before we break for weather and traffic, we have a little surprise for you. She survived the destruction of her home and the death of her family, only to be plucked from the wreckage of her house and kept as a hostage for two months, eventually losing her leg after being rescued. That's right, Jeannine LaRue is outside our trailer here at the Superdome, and she's giving a live and exclusive update on her recovery. Isn't that exciting, Monica?"

"That child is amazing, Peter. No doubt about it," replied Monica. "We'll speak to her and Dr. Stanley Bernstein, who has been instrumental in her recovery, right after we hear about this upcoming storm. Thank you for being with us this morning and *God Bless Louisiana!*"

Jones shook his head and paced back and forth through the weather report. Ninety seconds felt more like an eternity.

On the TV, the male anchor gushed again. "I can't believe how well you are walking already, Jeannine. It really is a miracle!"

And how straight her hair is, thought Curtis, *and the new Laura Ashley outfit . . .*

"Thank you, Peter," said the teen. "I thank God every night for this second chance He's given me."

"That's really good to hear. Your recovery seems to be going well, but how are you *feeling*?"

"I . . . have my moments," said Jeannine hesitantly. "But I'm learning to cope. Along with God, Dr. Bernstein has helped me so much. He's shown me so many different techniques that I feel like my mind is healing even faster than my body. Thank you, Dr. Bernstein."

"You're welcome, Sweetheart," said Dr. Bernstein, oozing into the conversation. "In fact, she is doing so well, we wanted to share some exciting news while we are here with you on WGNO."

"Now, Dr. Bernstein?" asked Jeannine.

"Let's bring out Officer Jones first, shall we? So we can all share together," said Dr. Bernstein with a smile.

"Well," laughed the host. "We do seem to have an empty chair on the set. A man who needs no introduction, one of many Heroes of Katrina and the man who rescued Jeannine—Officer Curtis Jones of the St. Dismas Parish Sheriff's Department!"

Everyone applauded as Jones walked onto the stage—everyone except Dr. Bernstein.

Jones settled into his chair with a wave and a half-hearted attempt at a smile. *What's the som'bitch up to,* he asked himself. Curtis looked over to Peter, but the man's back was already turned. The host was focused on Jeannine. Curtis tried to catch her eye, but she ignored him. *Maybe it's all the lights and the cameras.*

"Did you want to tell them or should I, Sweetheart?" Dr. Bernstein asked Jeannine once the polite applause faded away.

"Why don't you, Dr. Bernstein?" said Jeannine. "After all, it's your generosity that is making it all possible."

The exchange sounded rehearsed to Curtis's ears.

She sounds like one of those Disney kids. Vacant, yet always delighted to be at "The Happiest Place on Earth."

"How adorable!" said Peter, clapping his hands together. "Making what possible?"

"Well," began Jeannine with a smile and sideways glance at Dr. Bernstein. "There is a star-studded telethon planned live from Radio City Music Hall in New York next week."

"And," added the psychologist smoothly. "That's where we'll be launching my new talk show, called 'Dr. Stanley Wants to Help *You!*'"

I may vomit. Curtis looked at Jeannine, sitting perfectly still, a smile plastered on her face. It'd been nearly a month since he'd been allowed to see her. *What the hell has he done to you, J?*

Canned applause sounded around the studio and Dr. Bernstein looked directly into the camera and winked. "Our new website is up now—isn't the Internet a wonderful thing? And you should be able to see the link at the bottom of your screen, where you'll find an online form to not only request tickets but to request an interview to *appear on my show!*"

More canned applause.

"We'll be starting with a three-part special on Katrina, focusing on Jeannine's story and tying into the fundraiser."

"That sounds so exciting, Dr. Bernstein! And the show will be shown on ABC stations throughout the country, including our own WGNO *God Bless Louisiana!"*

There it is. Jeannine is his damn ticket to TV land! Som'bitch . . .

Curtis tried desperately to catch Jeannine's eye, to get any reaction from her at all. That's when he noticed Dr. Bernstein smiling and staring directly at him.

"And there's one more thing, Peter," Stanley said, and then paused in true showmanship fashion. "After today's show, I'm delighted to share with you all that Jeannine will be moving to New York, where I will sign adoption papers and become her new father!"

Canned applause. Both the hosts applauded and so did the TV crew. Even Jeannine was applauding, looking at Dr. Bernstein with her ice-blue eyes . . .

Dr. Bernstein held Curtis's gaze and continued talking. " . . . and I'll make sure she gets an education at the best private schools. I think we all can agree this is the life this young lady deserves after all she went through." Bernstein gave a crooked smile. "Isn't that right . . . officer?"

Applause and cheering continued around the studio. Jones sat, mouth agape. *This is why Bernstein wanted me here. He wanted to gloat, to flaunt the fact that he'd beaten me. I wanted to surprise Jeannine . . . Georgina said I shouldn't . . . I should involve her in the process . . . but the whole time this som'bitch shrink was planning to exploit her for a goddamn TV show . . .*

"That is just fantastic, Jeannine," gushed Peter. "We are all so happy, after all you've been through, that you are finally getting an opportunity at a *life*. Isn't that great, Officer Jones?"

The camera with the red light swung toward Jones. They all looked at him expectantly.

"I . . . yeah . . . sure," stuttered Curtis. "I mean, whatever Jeannine wants. Of course."

"Oh, come on, Officer," said Stanley, his voice taking on a sarcastic tone. "What sort of life could Jeannine possibly have in this city? Most of the residents who left aren't coming back, and your own police force can't handle the crime still rampant in the area. You think she'd rather stay here than go where the best medical and mental care is in the country? She'll have everything she could possibly ever want in New York."

"She won't have family," muttered Jones.

"What was that?" asked Bernstein, playing to the camera.

"Family. Jeannine won't have family."

"What are you on about, Officer? Jeannine's mother was locked away in a mental institution before Katrina, and her great aunt died during the storm. There are no LaRues left. Wait, you weren't thinking about *you*, were you?"

"Honestly? Yeah, my wife Georgina and I . . . "

"Well, Jeannine and I discussed her future. She is remarkably bright and mature for her age, wouldn't you agree, Officer? And when I proposed adoption—believe you me, I surprised even myself when I first said it aloud—she was all for it." Bernstein turned toward Jeannine. "What was it you said to me, my dear?"

"I said that I was afraid—afraid of where I would live, where I would go. Who would take care of me?" That unwavering smile never left her face.

She wouldn't even look at Curtis.

64

Bernstein applauded.

It was too much for Jones to take.

"Perhaps, Bernstein," said Curtis, rising from his chair. "if you took your pompous head out of your ass, you'd realize she has other people who care for her . . . "

"If you really did care for her, why didn't you tell her *you'd* take care of her?" Bernstein interrupted. "Poor, scared Jeannine. Someone had to step in, offer to be there for her, take care of her." Stanley flashed a toothy grin at the camera.

Out of sight of the viewing audience, Bernstein held up a middle finger toward Jones.

"You condescending som'bitch," said Jones. He dove at Bernstein with balled fists. Before the doctor could react, Jones cold-cocked him.

"Curtis!" screamed Jeannine. She tried to push Curtis away from Stanley, but she stumbled as her new prosthetic buckled.

She fell to the floor.

"Stop it!" she sobbed. "Stop it! Leave Uncle Stanley alone! I hate you!"

Curtis halted mid swing and looked at Jeannine— her tear-streaked face, her set jaw. Her eyes burning with fury.

She looked at Curtis for the first time today—her ice-blue eyes full of anger and pain.

Jeannine . . . hated him.

Stagehands rushed in to help the young survivor. Curtis felt himself pulled off "Uncle Stanley."

"We'll be right back," stammered Peter to the cameras.

EIGHT

THE BLACK ESCALADE traveled through New Orleans proper, the lights of the city turned to jewels by the rain drops that fell from the sky once again. Jeannine, Stanley, and the leggy brunette camera woman were sealed off from the driver via a blacked-out, soundproof partition. Jeannine felt like she was in a cave.

The young camera woman's thumbs flew across the screen of her smartphone. The handheld device provided the only light in the passenger compartment, painting everyone in a blue, sickly tint.

I'll bet she's updating her Instagram account, steamed Jeannine. *Stanley and his young women. Can't save them all, you pompous prick.*

"Why the hell did you follow me?" Jeannine finally asked from between clenched teeth. Visions. Dreams. And now this. The Universe certainly had a sick sense of humor.

"I'm worried about you," said Stanley's silky baritone. "As I said to you this morning back in New York before you stormed out, I can help you process

66

this—keep your head in the game for your pal Curtis Jones."

"You don't give a fuck about Curtis, so stop the bullshit." *So, Stanley doesn't know about the accident yet. Or maybe the Major was full of shit.*

"Now, Ms. LaRue," said Stanley's assistant, peering over the top of her glasses. "What Dr. Bernstein—"

"Sweetheart," spat Jeannine. "Why don't you just sit there and look pretty."

Jeannine could tell the woman was about to respond, but then she looked at Stanley. Jeannine didn't catch what silent communication passed between them, but the young assistant's lips nearly disappeared as she struggled to keep her mouth closed. Jeannine recognized the conflicted look on her face. She had worn that same look a while back.

Another young plaything for Stanley to tire of. I wonder if she's realized yet that her misplaced feelings were the result of nothing more than the sick, twisted manipulations of a . . .

"Why, I wonder, are you still so hostile toward women, Jeannine?" mused Stanley as his assistant's face went blotchy—even through her makeup. "Is it because you don't respect women who haven't had to overcome what you have? Or is it a jealousy thing—envious of those who haven't been traumatized?"

"Hmm, let's think about that. A or B," said Jeannine. "What about C? C being that she's one of your thralls and obviously hasn't yet figured out your games?"

The young woman looked up from her smartphone long enough to scowl at Jeannine.

"Maybe she hasn't copped on yet," amended Jeannine.

"Sir," interrupted a deep voice over the intercom. "There is a man standing on the highway."

"A man? What's he doing?" Stanley asked the driver.

"Just standing . . . oh, my God. He's missing an arm . . . "

"Go around him!" shouted Stanley, eyes widening in panic realization.

The tires squealed, then slipped on the slick pavement.

⚜

Roo's monster truck followed a few hundred yards behind the Major's car. Traffic on I-10 was light, and as they passed through Orleans Parish there was virtually no one else on the road—other than Bernstein's Escalade, the Major, and the dual cab F-350.

"Back off another couple hundred yards, Roo," said Curtis. "Pretty sure they are heading to the parish sheriff's office—let's not spook 'em."

"Maybe we can grab the armored truck if it's still there," murmured Gallow. "Maybe we can salvage the job."

"No way they got that thing out of the wall yet," said the Golem.

"Forget the job," growled Curtis.

"Months we planned this score," continued Gallow. "Do you know how much time and money we spent in prep alone?" Gallow was frustrated and Curtis couldn't blame him. They all were. And this murder frame-job couldn't have come at a worse time for all of them, including Curtis's silent partner. *I gotta tell 'em . . .*

"Look, I know you guys are pissed at me," began Curtis.

"Shit! What the fuck?"

At Roo's words, Curtis looked toward the road.

Roo hit the brakes and they all lurched forward in their seats.

Five hundred yards in front of them, Bernstein's Escalade lay on its side. Smoke, illuminated by the headlights of the Major's stopped car, billowed out of the ruined truck.

"What happened?" asked Gallow.

"We've made it to the wildlife preserve," shouted Curtis. "No lights, no witnesses. Nothing but highway in either direction. It's an ambush. And Jeannine could be hurt. We have to get her. Go, Roo!"

"What about the Major?" asked Roo.

"Fuck that asshole. Go. Go. Go!" said Curtis, pounding his fist on the dashboard.

The pickup lunged forward with a roar as Roo stomped on the gas. They quickly approached the ruined Escalade.

"You guys hold off the cops—" Curtis began.

Suddenly, the Major's car sped off, tires squealing.

"Wait, where are the cops going?" asked Curtis.

"What'n the hell?" said Roo. "The fuckin' cops didn't even stop!"

"Forget about them. Let's get to the wreck," said Gallow.

The pickup pulled up to the smoldering wreck. People already surrounded what was left of the Escalade.

"At least someone was willing to help," said Curtis.

"Jesus Christ!" shouted Roo "They're *not* helping!

They aren't even people! That's why the cops didn't stop! Weapons!"

Around the wreck, nearly half a dozen *things* clawed at the Escalade, breaking windows, pulling at ruined doors. In the lights of the pickup, horrific details became clear. Skin missing in patches, eyes milky white, mouths open in silent agony.

One guy didn't have an arm.

"What in all that is Holy . . . " began Curtis.

A woman's scream sent the shocked men into action.

Roo, Fernández, and Gallow aimed their shotguns at the zombie horde. The gun blasts reverberated around them. The humidity and dense overgrowth surrounding them amplified the sound. Bits of flesh flew off the attackers as shotgun pellets ripped at decaying bodies, but the creatures ignored the damage and steadfastly continued to rip apart the Escalade. The zombies—which was the only word Curtis's mind could find for them—pulled a dark-haired woman from the wreckage. All he caught was a glimpse of a face covered in blood. The woman screamed again, only to have the shrill sound of panic turn into a gurgle as the undead ripped out her throat.

"*Jeannine!*" screamed Curtis.

Shotguns went off again. Limbs disintegrated under the onslaught. Curtis and the Golem raced around the undead creatures. The woman lay face down on the ground, motionless in a pool of dark blood. Curtis knelt at her side and gently rolled her over.

The young camera woman's eyes were wide, terror-stricken, and her dead mouth frozen in a perpetual silent scream. Curtis felt ashamed as relief washed over him. *Not Jeannine.*

A moan from the truck made Curtis leave the dead girl and dodge the one-armed zombie to reach the shattered vehicle. The back door had already been pulled off by one of the undead. The thing was crawling inside the truck. Before Curtis could react, Charley "the Golem" Mouton let out a war cry and grabbed the creature by the legs. In seconds, the creature was pulled from the truck.

Curtis dove in to take its place, only to hear the low moan again.

The light from Roo's truck bounced off a balding pate.

The moan came from Bernstein.

Curtis spent an entire breath contemplating leaving the old fraud among the wreckage where he deserved to be. But then Curtis dragged him out of the truck.

"Fernández! Get over here! Man down!"

Curtis dove back into the wreck. He had to find her. She had to be okay.

The smell inside the SUV was nearly overpowering—burnt plastic, vomit, and blood. Curtis crawled through the mess, but he could find no one else. The partition in the front had shattered, and he already knew he'd find death there. Curtis had smelled death too many times in the past to ever forget that smell. In what remained of the front seats, two men lay twisted together, one with his head bashed in, the other with a crushed chest. Internal organs had splattered about the cab. Grey, ropy intestines wrapped around the victims.

Jeannine wasn't in the truck.

"She's not here!" he called. *Maybe she was thrown clear.*

"There is no one else out here," Gallow called back. "Bits of zonbi, that poor girl, and Bernstein."

Gallow thinks they're zombies, too. What the actual fuck is going on here?

"Zombies," muttered Curtis.

"It's zonbi in Creole," replied Gallow. "You should know this shit, boss."

"Is that som'bitch conscious?" Curtis asked Fernández, ignoring Gallow.

"Yeah, barely," replied Fernández. He'd been the team's medic during the war. "He needs a hospital. I've got the bleeding mostly stopped, but he has a broken femur and probably some internal injuries."

"Put him in the back of the pickup. We'll take him back to Roo's place," said Curtis. "Keep him stable for us, man."

"I'll do what I can," replied Fernández, then turned to the rest of the krewe. "Gallow! Roo! Give me a hand!"

Curtis took one more, quick look around the truck. *Where are you, Jeannine?* He didn't find her . . .

. . . but he found the Golem.

Charley lay in a heap surrounded by pieces of the undead. A shriveled zombie/zonbi hand clawed uselessly at the road next to him.

Curtis kicked the hand away, then fell to his friend's side. The Golem looked torn to shreds, but there was no blood to see. "Charley!" said Curtis. "How bad?"

"Grab . . . grab the tooth," was the reply. He smiled up at Curtis. "She'll be fine. Just make sure Roo gives me proper legs this time . . . "

The Golem's color faded, and he appeared to deflate, his body transforming into a fine powder that poured between Curtis's fingers.

"Charley!" croaked Curtis. *Roo hadn't been kidding when he'd given Charley his nickname—Golem. All this . . . shit, this magical bullshit . . . it was real.*

Curtis had always known it, deep down—especially when "she" had come to see him the night she'd found Jeannine. But he scoffed at magic. He'd always made fun of things that frightened him. That was his mind's way of coping—especially when the boys would talk about it. Ridicule. Feigned ignorance. Like a child hiding under the covers from the monster under the bed.

Curtis rooted around in the pile of dirt that had been his friend for a moment and came out with one tooth. He looked at it in shocked wonder.

"Jonesy! We got to git!" called Roo from where he stood on the driver's side sideboard of the truck. Gallow, still holding a shotgun, stood in the bed of the truck. That meant Fernández had Bernstein in the back seat.

Curtis carefully placed the tooth in his shirt pocket. Then, approaching the Ford, yanked the back door of the cab open a little harder than he meant to.

"He still alive?" Curtis called to Fernández.

"Yeah, and awake," replied Fernández. "He's in a lot of pain. I was about to knock him out with a bit of morphine."

"Yeah. Hold that thought." Curtis leaned into the television shrink's face. "Bernstein! Where is she?"

The man's eyes fluttered, then opened. "Hurts," he slurred.

"It's gonna hurt more if you don't tell me what happened."

"It . . . it was him. My fault," said the injured man, his eyes closing again.

"Him who? What happened? Stay with me, Bernstein! What the fuck happened to Jeannine?"

At the mention of his patient's name, Bernstein's eyes opened again. "Jeannine! He took her! That bastard took her!"

"Who took her?" Curtis grabbed the lapels of Bernstein's ruined suit.

"Guy. In the road. Swerved to miss him. Flipped. Crashed. Zonbis . . . zonbis. That means . . . Then someone else pulled her out, *he* pulled her out. Left the rest of us to his . . . his . . . dead minions . . . oh God."

"Who?"

"Papa Nightmare. He has Jeannine," sobbed Bernstein.

NINE

The Storm

HAD THE VISION *of her mother, Cassandra, on the roof been real? Had she, and maybe even Nana, somehow survived? How would she find them? How would they find her?*

These thoughts tormented her for hours as she struggled to stay alive, clinging to the shattered remains of the roof.

Rain sliced at her, mixing with her tears and blood. The storm was alive—a beast, a monstrous beast hell-bent on killing her. Wind tore around Jeannine, trying to throw her off balance into the waiting arms of the waters below and laughing at her like Cassandra had. Debris tore at her body, rending pajamas and flesh. This creature made of wind, rain, and fear had tasted Jeannine's blood and wanted more. It tried every trick to wear her down, to destroy her.

But she persevered.

The wind gave up first, quieting to an impotent breeze. Then, the needles of rain faded to a trickle. Despite the realization that she was alone, Jeannine called for her mother, for her Nana, her tears and blood flowing faster than the last of the rain. She wondered if now they might hear her.

The sun poked out hesitantly from behind the black, fast-moving clouds. Where once stood Jeannine's street—a place she had played with her friends and laughed over lemonade and popsicles— now rushed a new river. The body of Mrs. King, one arm missing, and wearing what was left of her favorite flower-patterned housecoat, bobbed in the churning waters. Jeannine's friend, Melinda, still moving feebly, held onto a dresser missing all its drawers and sinking into the rushing current.

Jeannine scrambled down the roof, calling Melinda's name as her friend floated closer. But before she could grab Melinda's leg, the girl disappeared under the brackish surface—pulled under by a massive black snake whose undulating muscles rippled and wrapped around her friend. Jeannine had never heard of such a creature in these parts, and her shock and disbelief turned to terror as the creature looked her dead in the eye and gave her a pointy-tooth smile, exactly as her mother had.

Jeannine scrambled farther up the roof.

A glint of sunlight off metal caught her attention. Two white men in an aluminum fishing boat with a tiny outboard motor putt-putted toward her. They waved as they made their way through the floating bodies. They looked filthy—one with matted and tangled hair that matched his greasy beard, the other wore a stained John Deere baseball cap with an uneven brim. She didn't care what they looked like, only that they were there and saw her. All Jeannine felt was relief.

"I'm saved," she thought.

BAYOU WHISPERS

Half drowned and now shivering uncontrollably in the chilled air, Jeannine called to God and Jesus, cursing Their names for taking her family away, but praising Them for her saviors in the aluminum boat.

But the two men were not sent by a benevolent God.

They weren't there to rescue her at all.

Present Day

"Wake, child," said a pleasant-sounding, deep voice.

Jeannine awoke, arms flailing, trying to hit anything within reach.

But, of course, nothing was in reach.

Laughter and a rhythmic splashing sound surrounded her.

She lay on an old wooden floor that smelled of mold and decay. She raised her head toward the sound of the loudest laugh.

A bare-chested man, who looked nearly seven feet tall and all muscle—wearing pinstriped pants, a matching jacket, a bowler hat, and expensive looking shoes—stared down at her with his arms crossed. He held, in the crook of one arm, some sort of walking stick topped with the skull of a small animal. He grinned—as did the dozen or so people standing around him.

Jeannine tried to clear the cobwebs and fog enough to kick her synapses into working again. *An accident. Stanley was being condescending again. A God-awful crash. People . . . pulling at her. That young woman . . . God, what happened to her? I shouldn't have been so nasty to that poor woman . . .*

Focus.

Jeannine focused on the pattern of splashes that continued unabated.

Control the fear. Don't let it control me.

When Jeannine had been kidnapped and held hostage after Katrina, she'd taught herself to shove all her emotions into a bottomless pit she'd created in her mind. It's also what made her a damn fine lawyer. It's what made her the "Ice Queen." The fear, the terror, the confusion. Any *feeling* that would keep her from thinking logically, she shoved into that mental pit. She was in control of herself now. That was the first step in figuring a way out of here.

She looked up at the big, bare-chested man.

He laughed again, as did most of the people with him. All except one man who wore sunglasses and stood off to the side. He was the only one not enjoying the show.

"You!" she spat.

She stood and moved to attack her would-be cab driver, but the floor shifted beneath her feet and she stumbled to the sound of metal striking wood. It was then she noticed the pain in her remaining ankle, the cold iron chain attached to a manacle and to the floor.

Jeannine tried to stand again, but the floor moved once more, seemingly determined to keep her down. A sharp pain shot through where her knee was attached to her prosthetic.

She fell, grimacing in pain.

Her tormentors tittered.

The sound of their laughter—a mirthless, cruel thing—brought back memories of being tied to a filthy bed. She struggled to put them back in that same pit with her fear. She was breathing hard and took a moment to calm herself. *You are the Ice Queen.*

"Unchain me, motherfucker, and we'll see who laughs then," she said, anger overriding fear.

The mirthful crowd went silent, expectant. They all looked with hungry eyes at the big bare-chested man in front of her.

"You have your mother's spirit, of that there can be no doubt," he said, caressing the stubble on his chin thoughtfully. "But, of course, if she had taught you The Way, you'd already be out of those chains, child. Perhaps you are not the threat the *mystères* think you are, hmm?"

Jeannine paused for a moment.

My mother? What the hell does this asshole know of my mother?

"Unchain me," Jeannine said again, grinding her teeth. "And I'll prove your complacency wrong."

"Not complacent, little one. Knowledgeable," replied the man. "First, I know who you are, but you do not know me."

"You're Papa Nightmare," Jeannine said without thinking. The sound of the name sent chills down her spine, but for the life of her, she didn't know why.

"Very good," said the man, nodding approval. The crowd surrounding them muttered quietly to themselves. "You know my *name*, but I still say you do not know *me*."

He waved his stick in the air and a circle of flame appeared from the now gaping mouth of the small skull. Sparks shot all over the floor. In the firelight, Jeannine saw it was made of old planks, peeling and splintered in places. The fire threw the crowd into sharp relief—and for the first time she noticed the men wore old-time uniforms. Some blue, others grey.

"Magic tricks don't impress me," she said. *Play for time. Find out what you can.*

"Hmm," mused Papa Nightmare again. "I am a Bokor. Do you know what that is?"

"No," lied Jeannine. *Nana told me.*

"I am a practitioner of Haitian Voudon magic, both light and dark."

"Voodoo, really?" Jeannine said, inserting a drop of sarcasm as her mind raced to remember all the things she had been told as a child. *Voodoo. Death magic. What had Nana said?*

Papa Nightmare ignored her tone.

"I am also the speaker for Ti Malice. Do you know of her?"

She shook her head no, meaning it this time. "Is she a Voodoo boogie-monster?"

"I can see you are truthful, if insolent," he replied. "Truth is not something many give freely, little one. You have gained my respect."

"If you respect me, let me leave."

Papa Nightmare gave her a rueful smile. "Even if I were so inclined, I assure you it is impossible at the moment."

"Why is that?"

"Because, right now you are aboard the *Sultana*, a damned ship with an extreme passion for death. The ship and I have . . . an understanding. Should you attempt to leave this vessel and the protection that being my guest affords you, the ship would collect your soul and you would join the rest of the passengers—forever."

TEN

Greenwood Cemetery Caretaker's Cottage
New Orleans
Papa Nightmare

CURTIS KNEW OF the legendary Voodoo witch doctor, of course. He was a local celebrity. He did magic for the tourists, all the while telling them stories of New Orleans's past. While he had the crowd's attention, his minions picked the pockets of the more inebriated audience members.

He was also in bed with the Cartel, providing safe passage for drugs and for people who wanted to come to the States illegally. If they could pay, of course. While Curtis's krewe didn't indulge in human trafficking or in drugs, Nightmare and Curtis were rivals of a sort. At least, Curtis liked to think so. In truth, his operation was small time compared to the self-proclaimed sorcerer.

Smaller than he'd thought, Curtis admitted to himself as he watched Fernández and Gallow carry the unconscious Stanley Bernstein into Roo's cottage.

Now, how the hell is the shrink mixed up in this?

"We need to get him to a doctor," grunted Fernández, as he and Gallow placed the man on the couch. "Pretty sure he's got more wrong with him than I can fix."

"I'm pretty sure, too," said Jones. "But that's exactly why we brought him here first. He might know where that charlatan took Jeannine. Wake him up."

Fernández dropped a backpack next to Bernstein and knelt down to work on him. Curtis pulled Roo aside.

"Here," said Curtis, holding out his hand.

"Charley's tooth?" asked Roo.

"Yeah. I don't understand all this. Will . . . this work?"

"Been workin' since the war," said Roo distractedly. "It's gonna take a day, though. I have a spare made, but the animation has to be done at dawn."

"Later. S'okay." Curtis deposited the yellowed bit of bone into Roo's hand. *Later doesn't really work for me, but I know that look.*

"Back in a tick," said Roo, already leaving the living room.

"Get that cat away from me!" shrieked a voice behind Curtis.

He turned to find the three-legged cat, Oliver, trying to settle in Bernstein's lap. The man struggled to push the animal away but yelped in pain.

"I need a doctor," said Stanley.

"Yes," agreed Curtis, "you do. But I have some questions for you first."

The former cop grabbed one of the wicker chairs from Roo's dining room and moved it close to the couch.

"You'll notice my boys are hovering near us," began Curtis. "Don't worry about any knives or guns they may or may not have on their person."

"I'm not saying a goddamn thing to you," Bernstein replied.

"Meow!" said Oliver, settling on the arm of the couch, his big golden eyes fixed on Bernstein.

"I'm allergic to cats," mumbled Bernstein.

"Oh, that's the least of your problems. Let's start with something more important. Where did Nightmare take Jeannine?"

"Who?"

Gallow laughed. "Oh, dear," he mocked. "Memory problems. Want me to . . . ?"

"Nah, I've got this," said Curtis, poking Bernstein in his broken ribcage. The man screamed.

"I don't know! I don't know where he is!"

"Ah, so you *do* know him." Curtis held a finger an inch above Bernstein's chest.

"Yes! Yes, all right, yes. I know him. Met him when I first came to this city."

"When you met Jeannine."

"Yes."

Oliver began to purr loudly and closed his eyes.

Bernstein looked at the cat, then coughed, spasming with pain. Blood dotted his spittle.

"Oh, that's not good," mocked Curtis. "Cut lip? Or did you bite your tongue during the crash? Or did a piece of rib splinter and cut into a lung?"

"You're an asshole." Bernstein coughed. More blood.

"I am what you made me," shrugged Curtis. "Jeannine. Nightmare. What's the connection?"

Bernstein closed his eyes, slipping back into unconsciousness. His color didn't look good—greyish-green. The blood was definitely from his lungs. Bright red meant plenty of oxygen. He'd die if he didn't get help soon. As Curtis thought that, Fernández said it. He wanted to call an ambulance.

Curtis looked at Fernández. He knew Fernández wouldn't do anything until Curtis gave the go ahead.

Shit.

Curtis didn't want this prick's death on his head. He nodded toward Roo's phone—an old Princess handset mounted on the wall.

Fernández nodded back and left the room.

Oliver gave a loud hiss. Bernstein woke with a jerk and lashed out with his foot at the animal. But, even missing a back leg, the cat was still faster than the injured psychologist.

"Stanley," said Curtis. "We both want the same thing: Jeannine's safe return. If you know Nightmare, you know how dangerous he is. Give me something to go on and we'll get you to the hospital."

Bernstein coughed wetly and looked at Jones. His eyes were watery and slightly yellow. *Maybe a damaged liver. He needed a doctor now. You will die here if you don't give me something.*

"How about this one," offered Curtis. "Where were you taking Jeannine?"

Bernstein stared at Curtis for a full minute.

Finally, the injured man blinked.

"Sheriff's office. The Major wanted to speak with her."

"He was at the airport . . . "

"And Jeannine blew him off. The Major knew she would. I called him from my plane on the way down. I agreed to help him, to get her to the Major."

"Why?"

Bernstein shook his head. "Jeannine wasn't

supposed to come back to this place. I failed. I was supposed to keep her out of New Orleans."

"I'll ask again," said Curtis. "Why?"

"Orders. He had Jeannine's phone tapped. Canceled her calls for a ride share."

"He? The Major?"

Bernstein nodded.

That wasn't good. If the Major tried to speak with Jeannine and was shut down, then sent in Bernstein . . .

"It was a setup," said Gallow.

Curtis nodded. Oliver brushed against his leg and he absently scratched behind the animal's ear.

"I told you, I'm allergic!" yelped Bernstein. "Get that thing away from me."

"Let me tell you a story. This cat was scrounging around some of the dumpsters behind Gallow's restaurant a couple years back. Injured leg, dirty. All alone. Sound familiar?"

Bernstein swallowed and closed his eyes.

"Roo and I found him. Took him to the vet. The poor thing's leg had to come off. How about that? Is that familiar?"

Bernstein turned his head away.

"I'd do anything for this cat." Oliver jumped into Curtis's lap, hissed once at Stanley, and then began kneading Curtis's leg. "Cost thousands in vet bills. A lot of rehab. A lot of training. Time and money—for a cat."

The cat jumped to the floor.

Curtis leaned over to whisper in Stanley's ear.

"Imagine what I would do for a human being I cared about. Imagine what I would do to someone who mistreated her. One chance, Stanley. Where did Nightmare take her?"

"A boat. He has a boat. I heard him say something about a trip down the ol' Miss."

Curtis nodded. At that moment, two paramedics came into Roo's cottage wheeling a stretcher. One was a heavy-set man with beads of sweat on his brow, the other tall and skinny.

"Harve, Legs," said Curtis, greeting them both. "VIP treatment for this one. But keep him on ice for a while."

"Sure boss," said Legs, the tall one.

They lifted Bernstein onto the stretcher, set up an IV, and wheeled him away without another word. Little Dave escorted them out.

"Thanks, Fernández," called Curtis.

"He knows where we are and *who* we are," grumbled Gallow.

"The boys'll keep him on ice until I tell them not to," replied Curtis. "Anybody know about a boat?"

"What boat?" piped in Roo as he came back into the cottage.

"Nightmare took Jeannine to a boat, maybe," said Curtis. "At least toward the river, according to TV guy. Any ideas?"

Roo's black skin seemed to turn grey.

"A boat?"

"What do you know, man?"

"Look, Jonesy. I know you don't put a lot of stock in Voudon . . . and I know you won't believe me . . . "

"I fought a bunch of dead things tonight and gave you a tooth for a friend of mine you're planning on bringing back to life at dawn. Pretty sure I'll believe you now."

"Rumor has it that Papa Nightmare has gained a lot of influence in recent years. Walks in powerful circles. As a Bokor, he has dominion over the dead . . . "

"Saw enough at the accident scene to believe you, Roo. I'm not sure how I feel about this shit but based on the lack of reaction from the rest of the boys, I guess they've taken you at your word longer than I have. We're gonna talk about that. But for now, I'm listening."

Roo took a second, then nodded. "Ever hear of the *Sultana?*"

Curtis thought for a moment. "Yeah. Big sidewheel steamboat. Wasn't there a fire or something?"

Roo nodded again. "One of the biggest maritime disasters in U.S. history. In 1865, the ship was traveling from St. Louis to New Orleans, carrying way too many people. Paroled Civil War vets, mostly. She exploded outside of Memphis—over a thousand people were killed."

"Hell, I didn't know that," said Curtis. "What does this ship have to do—?"

"I'm getting there, big guy," said Roo. "The damn thing burned to the waterline. Bodies everywhere. It was a mess."

"How come it's not, like, *Titanic* famous?"

"It was April of 1865. There was a news story much bigger in the press. Lincoln had just been shot in the head."

"Okay, so this is a reconstructed ship? Where do we—"

"No, you don't get it, man. It's *the* ship. The *Sultana*. It and its dead passengers were given to Papa Nightmare as a gift, of sorts."

"Of sorts?"

"Yeah. See, when something is the cause of so much death, so much pain, it can gain a sort of . . . sentience."

"I'm not going to even pretend to understand that right now. Where can we find Nightmare's 'gift'?"

Roo shook his head. "I don't know."

"Wait," said Curtis. "You said a gift. From who?"

"Whom. Rumor has it that it was given to Papa Nightmare by a Haitian deity—called a Loa—by the name of Ti Malice."

"Oh, for fuck's sake!" spat Curtis. "Now we're dealing with necromancy and gods? What's next, a ring of doom?"

"See?" said Roo. "I knew you wouldn't believe me."

ELEVEN

Aboard the Sultana

T HE GHOSTS AND PAPA NIGHTMARE left her alone.

With no one to see her, judge her, mock her, Jeannine could remove the mental armor she always wore.

She began trembling—whether it was due to the cold or fear, she didn't know. Next came the tears. At first, she tried to hold it all back. But like the levees the day she was reborn, the mental barriers didn't last long.

Rebirth. Something she hadn't thought about in a very long time.

She remembered the aluminum boat her "rescuers" had sat her in. The smell of wet dog surrounded her as soon as the men sat her down between them. But there was no dog in the little motorboat.

Water sloshed at her feet—but that hadn't mattered one bit. She was soaked from hours of enduring the storm.

The feeling of elation at being plucked off the roof by those rough-looking men. Unshaven, smelling of body odor and tobacco, they both had wide grins showing stained teeth and gaps where other teeth had been.

The fingernails. She noticed them next. Long, broken bits of keratin holding dirt as black as night. Their clothes too small for one, too large for the other, and well worn, stinking of swamp—and worse.

Mosquitos. Swarming over and around her yet leaving the men alone as if even these foul insects had standards.

Both men stared at her. Filthy grins frozen on their faces.

"Th-thank you so much for saving me," she said.

They didn't reply. The one with the John Deere cap stared at her, while the other with the long, matted hair and beard piloted the boat across the flooded neighborhood.

"Where are you taking me?" she asked. "Is there any place not flooded?"

"Don'tcha worry yer pretty little head none," said matted-hair.

"I'm hungry," she said, looking away.

The one with the cap hit her.

It wasn't a slap. Nor was it the light sort of spanking she'd received from her Mama.

He had punched her in the jaw.

She almost toppled out of the boat. She began to cry. The man with the cap hit her again.

"Don't hurt her mouth none," said matted-hair. "I have a use for that."

They both laughed as Jeannine cried.

Laughter and tears.

Jeannine focused on the present. She was still in the *Sultana's* dining room, but no longer alone.

The ghoul sat in a rickety deck chair in front of her. He wore sunglasses and played a mournful blues melody on a beaten up, dented saxophone.

"You are stronger than him," hissed Easy Street, as he lowered the mouthpiece of the horn. "Fight it. He has been told to break you, and he will show you your worst nightmares."

Jeannine laughed. A wet-sounding sickly noise that made the dead musician put the sax down altogether.

"I've lived worse nightmares than he can show me," said Jeannine.

"*That's* what he'll key in on," replied Easy. "You think those thoughts you were just havin' showed up in your head randomly? No, he's fiddlin' with your noggin. Fight him."

"Why the hell do you care, maggot-eyes?"

"Yeah, okay. That was a bit o' drama, I admit. I was tryin' to scare you off comin' down here."

"That what Papa Nightmare sent you to New York for?"

"Yes and no," said Easy Street. "His goals and mine are different."

"See, I think you're full of ecto-bullshit, ghost-boy," replied Jeannine. "If Papa Nightmare can see into my head, that means he's watching you as well. So why would you even hint at a competing agenda?"

Easy Street said nothing. He reached behind his chair, pulled out the battered sax case Jeannine had seen in his cab, and began to disassemble his horn.

"You have a lot of your mother in you, that's fo' damn sure," he said finally. "Most normal people, having discovered spirits were real and they was being held prisoner on a ghost ship, would react way different than you. Think about that as Papa Nightmare plays in yo' head, little lady."

When he stood, the deck chair was suddenly gone. He looked at her through those dark glasses, shook his head once, turned, and walked away.

He faded into a mist that sprang up as he left. The mist dissipated as fast as it appeared.

Thunk.

Something metallic hitting up against heavy wood. Jeannine didn't grow up surrounded by water and did not know that sound. She squinted at the place where Easy Street had been as a new shape took form. It rocked slowly until enough of the image came together that it made sense to her.

A small aluminum boat.

The smell of the swamp flooded Jeannine's nostrils. Other smells, too. Dog hair.

Human body odor.

A slow laugh rolled over the sounds of the boat nudging the dock.

"Nice ta see you again, little lady. You's all grown an' shit, ain't ya?" The question dripped with pure maliciousness.

"She still smells good, though," said another voice. "Don'tcha, little lady?"

She could see two figures in the boat. Two men. She couldn't breathe—she knew who these men were.

"We used to have fun together. Why don'tcha come play with us like ya used to?" asked the one with matted hair.

The chains attached to Jeannine's good ankle slithered away, freeing her to stand. She stood, favoring the prosthetic leg. There was a little pain, but nothing she hadn't dealt with before. The leg would require some adjustments, but for now, it held.

She could probably hobble to the railing and throw herself overboard. But would that kill her? Or worse, make her a part of this voyage of the damned?

"Please, for the love of God Almighty, please try and escape. We wanna catch you!" said the figure with the ball cap.

You have a lot of your mother in you, that's fo' damn sure.

Images flooded into Jeannine's head. Sensations more than images.

Her mother.

The warmth of a bed.

A smile filled with love.

Story time.

Singing.

A hymn, one she knew by heart so long ago, but had forgotten. Taught to her by . . .

. . . her Nana? No—her mother! She remembered her mother's voice!

Her mother. When she loved her. Before she changed.

When peace like a river, attendeth my way,
When sorrows like sea billows roll
Whatever my lot, thou hast taught me to say
It is well, it is well, with my soul
It is well
With my soul
It is well, it is well, with my soul.

R.B. WOOD

A sense of calm, of peace, wrapped around her.

All those stories about her family and dark magic—she thought Nana had made them up to entertain her as a small child. She thought they were stories, nothing more. She could feel her mother's voice; it permeated the ship's wooden timbers and planks.

The shadow men in the boat covered their ears.

I was wrong. Look at them! The shadows . . . they can hear Mama's singing!

The two men began screaming.

Her mother's voice, always so beautiful, better than the voices on the radio. Jeannine willed her mother's song to soar louder.

The shadow men fell. They, and the surrounding darkness, melted like oil oozing off a pan. It oozed away from Jeannine. The lights grew brighter and brighter.

The sound of a heavy vehicle skidded on pavement, doors opened and closed.

The warmth of the rain. The hardness—not of deck planking, but of blacktop.

Strong hands grabbed her. Lifted her up.

"You're safe," whispered a voice from her past. "I promise."

"About fucking time you showed up, Curtis," mumbled Jeannine. "This means I'm either dead or that Major prick lied to me."

"You're not dead, and always assume the prick is lying to you."

"'Kay," she slurred.

Light and the dark both took her then, and she fell limp in Curtis's arms into a troubled sleep.

TWELVE

Greenwood Cemetery Caretaker's Cottage
New Orleans

SHE'D APPEARED IN the middle of the road, damp and muddy, but alive. Roo tried to explain how the *Sultana* could travel on any existing and past waterway—and certainly the bit of road they'd been on was near enough to the river. But no one could explain to Curtis why Jeannine had appeared *exactly* where the krewe was at *exactly* the right time.

Gallow wanted to bring her to a hospital, but Curtis, not trusting any government institution, had insisted they go back to Roo's safe house. Curtis carried her into the caretaker's cottage himself but refused to lay her on the couch that Stanley-the-asshole had occupied barely an hour earlier. He carried Jeannine up the stairs to the little spare room across from the master.

The room was just big enough for a creaky twin bed with fresh sheets. Roo never knew when a member of the krewe would be sleeping one off at his place, so he kept the bed at the ready.

"She'll be out for a while," said Roo. "I think we all could use a few hours of shut-eye."

"The Major'll figure out where we are," said Curtis, an unreadable expression on his face as he watched Jeannine sleep.

"No, he won't. This place can't be found unless I want it to be."

"More mumbo-jumbo?"

Roo gritted his teeth and hissed, "Downstairs. Now."

Roo turned and shuffled out. Curtis watched him go, gave Jeannine one last look, then followed down the stairs. *Gotta tell 'em.*

Gallow and Fernández sat on the couch, speaking intently in a hushed tone, stopping as Curtis reached the ground floor.

They both guiltily looked at him, eyes shifting from Curtis, to their shoes, and back again.

"You guys wanna share?" asked Curtis.

"Of course they don't," snarled Roo, turning on Curtis. "But I sure as shit do."

"Roo, I . . . "

"Zip it, *boss*," said Roo with a sarcastic emphasis on the title. "They're pissed that the first big score we spent months planning was thrown out the window for a woman who a decade ago as much as said she hated your living, breathing guts. They're amazed you can still question any of the voodoo magic you've seen tonight—and it's not just tonight that you've questioned us, it's going back to Desert Storm! And finally, they are wondering if they should just turn you and Jeannine over to the Major and be done with this mess."

Roo rounded on the two red-faced men. "I miss anything, boys?"

They both looked anywhere but at either Roo or

Curtis. The silence was as thick as the humidity and smelled nearly as bad as the Mississippi at low tide.

Finally, Curtis nodded.

"Okay, you're right. All of you," he said as he held out his hands, palms open. "I'll tell you what. Let's clear the air. Right here, right now. I'll answer any questions you have, and in turn I'll listen to your story about magic. I'm ready to hear what y'all have to say."

Gallow—never one to miss an opportunity to leverage a situation—immediately asked, "What is it with you and this woman?"

Curtis looked at him, searching for the words. He grabbed one of Roo's wooden chairs, turned the back toward the couch, and sat down, facing his krewe.

"Grab the other chair, Roo," said Curtis. "This night's about to get longer."

1 November 2005
St. Dismas General Hospital, ICU Waiting
Room

The teenager was in surgery to have her leg amputated.

His partner, Randy, had gone back to the office to take care of the paperwork. The Major had called three times before Curtis had shut off his phone.

An untouched now cold cup of coffee sat on a table next to Curtis. An unread *Sports Illustrated* sat open on his lap, celebratory Chicago White Sox players on the cover.

He'd seen amputations before. On the battlefield. He still heard the screams.

Charley's were the loudest in his memory.

❧

An IED had caught the right passenger side of the Humvee, flipping the vehicle twice. Roo, the gunner, had been tossed like a ragdoll. Develin and Davis had caught the blast, the latter's face blown off. Curtis had found the bloody mask of skin afterward, about twenty meters up the road, still recognizable.

Develin had died trying to stuff his grey, ropey intestines back into the hole in his side.

Charley had taken a nasty piece of shrapnel in his leg. It had cut an artery.

When Curtis had arrived at the wreckage, he'd located Charley by the blood fountaining out of his wound. Curtis had tied a tourniquet up by Charley's crotch and temporarily stemmed the blood. Then the medic had arrived—Curtis didn't remember the kid's name and he wouldn't have to: a week after the IED incident the medic would be taken out by a sniper.

The no-named medic had torn the rest of the bloody fabric from Charley's pants, only to discover shredded meat where a leg had once been.

Charley had screamed.

"I'm gonna need you to hold him," was the only thing No-name had ever said to him.

Shouts of "clear" had gone up around them as the rest of the Army Rangers vacated the area.

As No-name had taken out a bone saw, Roo had hobbled up to them.

"Charley! Oh my God!" he'd exclaimed. Roo had fallen to his knees by his friend just as No-name began to saw.

The screams had been primal, animalistic. The

sound an animal makes when it's being eaten alive by a predator . . .

❧

A hand on his shoulder took Curtis from one nightmare to another.

Dr. Broussard had that look of detached concern all doctors master by the end of their residency.

"She made it through surgery just fine," said the doctor. "She'll be asleep for a while and on a drip for the pain for a few days."

"When . . . " Curtis mentally kicked himself as he struggled to bridge this new reality with the one from his memory. "When can I see her?"

"She'll be back in her room in ICU in a couple of hours."

"Thanks, Doc."

Broussard nodded once, then left.

Curtis had always considered hospital waiting rooms to be haunted places. The amount of misery and anxiety those rooms saw could only be compared to the deep sadness surrounding funeral homes.

Or the despair that slithered around battlefields.

Sensitive people—psychic sensitives—perceived these spaces. Those who didn't know of their own sensitivity just felt a sense of restlessness. A need to leave the area.

True sensitives could see more than normal humans.

Which is why Curtis didn't jump when a woman's voice said, "Hello, Curtis."

He sighed.

She had first appeared along with the 9-1-1 call

about a woman menacing a child with a machete, in 2005 before Katrina. He and Randy had found her, naked, covered in cuts inflicted on herself with that damn blade. She was foaming at the mouth, laughing maniacally, and sitting in a puddle of her own urine while slicing little bits of flesh off her arms. It had taken both his and Randy's tasers to bring down the woman.

The child, a girl, had been sitting on a bed—she'd gone into some sort of shock.

This was the first time he'd met Jeannine, though he hadn't known her name yet. For her part, the child would never remember meeting him that night.

Once an ambulance had taken them away—the girl to be patched up, as she'd sustained a few deep wounds from her mother's machete, the mother to be patched up, then whisked off to a mental hospital, where she'd eventually meet her own fate, handcuffed to her hospital bed during Katrina—Curtis had gone home to pour himself a triple.

He was on his third Jack Daniel's when the spirit of the mother had shown up the first time. It was just like now, here in the hospital waiting room.

The air went still as the sounds of the hospital faded to nothing. The temperature dropped and Curtis gave an involuntary shiver.

"'lo Cassandra, you evil bitch. Was wondering when you'd show up," he said without looking in the direction of the voice. "Your daughter is out of surgery. Gonna be fine, but minus a leg."

"I know. I've been singing to her."

"I did what you asked. I found her where you said I would."

"And I must ask you to continue to watch over her. She "woke," Curtis. It will be bad for her now."

He stood, suddenly angry. "Why me? Why do I have to do this now? I would have . . . "

"I know, Dear-heart. But she wasn't yours. I couldn't have asked you then."

"But now?"

"She has no one else, Curtis. No one. There are forces at play that will try to take her, corrupt her. That must not happen. She is a sensitive like you. Like I was. But so much more. Her power is on a scale you can't possibly imagine. She needs you."

"I promised you I would take care of her," said Curtis, sitting heavily back down. Tired. So damn tired.

"Then I am satisfied you will. Goodbye, Dear-heart."

Curtis was again alone in the waiting room. No one heard his sobs.

⚜

"That's one hell'uva story, you son of a bitch. Your blind ignorance of Voodoo . . . *faked? This whole fucking time?*"

Roo had come out of his chair. His hands were clenched into fists by his side.

"It's not Voodoo, what I can do. It's . . . a sort of a sixth sense," replied Curtis.

"You speak to spirits, Curtis," said Gallow quietly. "That sounds a bit like Voodoo to me."

"It's not," said Roo and Curtis at the same time.

"Controlling the dead, reanimation. That's the dark portion of Voudon," said Roo, his voice trembling with barely controlled anger. "That's what

Papa Nightmare does. I don't know what Curtis is doing."

"It's like a séance without the Ouija board," said Curtis, glaring back unblinkingly at Roo. "And I won't apologize to any of you over it. I didn't want this. You think I like speaking with the dead and mostly dead? It's not a fuckin' picnic, boys."

"So, you spoke with Cassandra. What else haven't you told us?" asked Gallow.

"That's an interesting question," said a voice from the stairway. "I'd kinda like to hear an answer to that myself, motherfucker."

Jeannine was awake.

THIRTEEN

Aboard the Sultana

"IS SHE AWAY?" asked Papa Nightmare, still naked from the waist up, sitting relaxed in the captain's chair on the bridge of the doomed paddle wheeler.

"Yes, Papa. As you foresaw," a ghoul in the uniform of the Confederacy replied.

"Very well. Bring him to me."

The ghoul bowed to Papa Nightmare and then hurried from his master's presence. A rustling breeze lazily, almost erotically, brushed the Voudon priest's face. The breeze was warm, like the breath of a lover speaking of lustful needs.

"Yes, my lady," rumbled Papa Nightmare. "All is well. She is strong enough, when properly motivated. I just need a little more time."

The wind suddenly howled, bringing the smell of death and decay. A piece of decking came loose and struck Papa Nightmare on the cheek.

"Patience, lord," he said, and the wind subsided as suddenly as it had risen.

He reached to his cheek and found blood. He slowly licked the warm crimson fluid from his finger. "Patience. It is happening exactly as I expected."

The whisper returned to its lustful timbre.

"And I, you," replied Papa Nightmare.

Two soldiers, this time in Union blue uniforms, dragged in a sorry-looking spirit wearing sunglasses. They unceremoniously dropped him at the feet of Papa Nightmare.

"Leave us," Papa Nightmare said to the soldiers.

On this ship, even the dead had things to fear. Both soldiers left without a word.

Papa Nightmare turned his attention and gaze to the pitiful figure in front of him.

"Hello, Easy Street. Now that you have seen her again, what do you think of our little *plaçage*?"

"Papa Nightmare, please," sobbed the old jazzman.

"Oh, my favorite musician, my court jester. Your job was a simple one. Keep her away from N'Orleans. You couldn't even do that right, could you? But, of course, I knew you'd fail."

Papa Nightmare stood. He reached down and in one quick motion grabbed Easy Street by his hair and yanked his entire body off the deck so they could look into each other's eyes.

Except, of course, Easy Street didn't have any eyes.

"This means punishment. Even if it is foretold, you still failed me. Failed *her*. We demand . . . entertainment."

"God, no . . . " pleaded Easy Street.

"Your feeble God does not sail with us this evening, jazzman."

The ghost screamed.

Even the dead had things to fear.

BAYOU WHISPERS

⚜

Lulu White's Saloon, Basin Street, New Orleans
1946

It was hot, damn hot. But the music was hotter.

The locals were still celebrating Mardi Gras three weeks on and Lulu White's place had been open nonstop since Fat Tuesday. Really, it had been hopping since the end of the war and Mardi Gras was just the most recent of excuses.

On stage, a woman calling herself "Blue Sue Barker" fronted a band with no name. And Easy Street loved her. "Loved" might be too strong of a word. Perhaps lust was better, even more so since it was his favorite of the deadly sins.

At the end of the last set, he'd had Sue nearly agreeing to go out back with him for a quickie, but he didn't have a frog skin, so back on stage she went.

"She wouldna' even give you a blowie, huh, Easy?"

Fat Freddie—his trumpet player bandmate and a dope head—had sidled up to Easy at the bar. He smelled of cheap whiskey, reefer, and a cheap hooker or two. Sweat streamed from his scalp, pooling in the folds of his neck, staining what Easy knew to be his only good shirt.

Easy turned away from Freddie, focusing all his attention on his empty scotch.

"Why you set yo' sights so high, my man?" Fat Freddie continued. He never could take a hint. "There's plenty o' girls willing for not a lot o' coin. You can get seconds. Or fifths."

Easy Street shook his head. "Not my scene, man. You dig?"

"I've got some top-dog giggle-smokes, man. C'mon outside for a minute," replied Freddie.

Easy grabbed his nearly empty glass, held it up to Fat Freddie, and said, "I'm covered."

The trumpeter shrugged his shoulders, turned, and pushed through the crowd toward the exit. Easy soon lost him in the haze-filled room.

Applause rippled through the crowd as Blue Sue took to the piano. The crowd went wild as she plunked out the first chords of "Just One of Those Things." She held Easy's eyes as she throatily and slowly crooned:

It was just one of those things
Just one of those crazy flings
One of those bells that now and then rings
Just one of those things.

Easy matched her gaze, enjoying the silent, dirty conversation in front of scores of people, when he felt someone touch his arm.

"Easy," said the bartender, placing a muddy-looking drink in front of him and nodding his head toward the stage. "From the lady."

The jazzman grabbed the drink with a smile and turned toward the stage. Blue Sue still stared at him, echoing his toothy grin.

Easy held up the glass to her and downed it in one go.

It took a strength of will he didn't know he had not to puke up the drink right there. *Jesus, Mary, and Joseph, what sort of drink had she sent?* Of course, he made a show of smacking his lips, his grin frozen on his face. He knew he had to put on a brave face to get her panties off. Blue Sue wouldn't suffer no weak-ass sax player. He felt like Fat Freddie as sweat poured off his forehead and dripped from the tip of his nose. But he held that grin. For her. For Blue Sue.

Her own smile never wavered and Easy thought he'd gotten away with it. He might still get laid after all. But his most immediate concern was to empty his stomach of whatever that drink was. As Sue's song finished to raucous applause and hoots, Easy made his way outside. He made it three whole steps before the contents of his stomach splattered on the dirt alleyway.

Easy leaned against the wall of the bar. He could hear muffled laughter and conversations. He couldn't make out the words, but he imagined all sorts of hedonistic discussions going on.

Just another night at Lulu's.

He pulled a handkerchief from his pocket and wiped bits from his mouth and chin. A shot of whiskey would fix him up. He had another set to perform after Blue Sue finished . . .

"Hey sugar, you okay?"

Sue was there in the alley with him. Easy quickly stuffed the sodden piece of cloth into his pocket.

"Yeah, baby. I'm good," he said. "Needed a bit o' air before my set, know what I mean?"

She moved in close, pinning him against the wall. She rubbed her leg against his crotch. "Oh, I know what you mean, sugar. Was thinkin' 'bout you while I was on stage. I know you've gotta go on in a sec, but how about I . . . "

Her hand was on him. Suddenly, he didn't care about the pool of sick or the next set.

"Yeah, baby," he said breathlessly. "You like what yo' feelin'? It's all for you . . . "

"Oh, don't I know it, Dear-heart," purred Blue Sue. She locked eyes with Easy, smiled, and slowly began to sink to her knees.

And that's when Fat Freddie shot him in the head.

Twice, once above each eye.

The sound was muffled by the partiers inside. Easy tried to say something, but his mouth moved silently. Both his eye sockets—eyes now missing from the impact of the bullets—oozed blood while crimson also streamed from the perfectly matching round holes the 32 slugs had made.

The jazzman slid down the wall, dead even before his heart stopped pumping.

Blue Sue stood, looking down at Easy. His blood spackled her stage dress. She tsked.

"I liked his eyes, Freddie. Now I have a servant with no eyes, you fat turd."

Still standing in the alley over Easy's body, Freddie replied, "I'm sorry, Ca—"

"It's Blue Sue, tonight, you idiot," the singer hissed, "Clean up this mess . . . I'm about to be asked to go back on stage."

❧

The specter of Easy Street lay curled up in a ball, sobbing at Papa Nightmare's feet. The Voudon priest squatted near the dead jazzman and put his hand on his shoulder, almost in a brotherly fashion.

"I do not understand why you weep so," said Papa Nightmare. "It is a privilege to be killed by our sleeping Ti Malice. You were chosen to serve her for all eternity. It is a privilege! Those tears of yours shouldn't be selfish and sad. They should be tears of joy. You shall relive your death again and again until you see the joy in the experience for yourself. Until you can face our master when she wakes from her slumber."

Easy Street let out a long, low noise like a mortally wounded animal.

Papa Nightmare returned to his captain's chair and addressed one of his Civil War ghouls.

"Has she stopped?"

"Yes, Papa. They are on the grounds of an old cemetery, according to our informant."

"Excellent. Change course and prepare the others."

FOURTEEN

Greenwood Cemetery Caretaker's Cottage
New Orleans

CURTIS LOOKED AT Jeannine standing on the first step that led up to Roo's attic conversion.

He finally had a moment to process that Jeannine was back in town. She was really here.

And she was pissed.

A mix of emotions overwhelmed him. He wanted to throw his arms around her and tell her he was sorry. He wanted to yell at her for going off with that asshole Bernstein all those years ago. He wanted to laugh, to cry. To scream. He wanted to tell her he'd protect her, and it would be all right.

But all he could do was to remember to breathe.

"Well, it's a pretty long and convoluted story," he finally said. It even sounded lame to his ears.

"I'm used to listening to long, convoluted stories from defendants," replied Jeannine. "I think I'd like to hear it."

"Jeannine . . . it's been so long, couldn't we just . . . ?"

"No," she said flatly. "I have some questions, Curtis, and I'm going to get answers first before we get all teary-eyed and try to make up."

You're not gonna like the answers, J. But I'll tell you everything.

Everything.

He sighed.

"Ask your questions," he said to the room.

"Jonesy," said Gallow, and the ex-cop heard the barely controlled panic in his voice. "The cops know where Roo lives. Do we have time for a Q&A session?"

"Roo said that real folk can't find this place unless he wants them to. So according to what you all believe, we'll be fine here. Plus, she's waited a long time for answers." Turning to Jeannine, Curtis said, "Go ahead. I'll answer what I know."

Jeannine sat on the stairs, arms crossed.

"Why did that cop tell me you were dead?" she asked.

"I didn't know that he did," said Curtis truthfully. "The Major—he's always throwing people off balance. That's what he does best. Blindsides you with information—true or not—then watches what happens."

"But it was such an obvious lie, he must have known I'd find out," said Jeannine slowly, in that distant voice she had when she was "piecing together a cogent argument," as she used to say.

"He was probably trying to get you to go with him and was hoping the shock of telling you I was dead would lower your defenses."

"Well, that fucking plan failed. I'm an officer of the court, why would he screw with me?"

"Best guess? I think he's taking orders from the same person Stanley was," said Curtis.

"Papa Nightmare?" piped in Roo.

"Papa Nightmare is working for somebody, too. Someone named Ti Malice," said Jeannine.

Roo grabbed a kitchen chair and sat down heavily. "That's . . . not good."

"Why?" asked Jeannine. "Who is this person?"

"She's not a person. She's a Loa. And sometimes she's a he. Ti Malice is a trickster, a charlatan of sorts."

"So Loas are gods," said Jeannine.

"No," replied Roo. "They are, for lack of a better term, intermediaries between God and mankind."

"They?"

"Oh, yes," said Roo. He had a manic gleam in his eye. "There are many Loa. Ti Malice is in direct conflict with Tonton Bouqui, for example . . . "

"Skip the lesson, Roo," said Curtis, recognizing his friend's wind-up all too well.

"Right. Sorry."

"So, you think Papa Nightmare, the Major, and Stanley are all working for this Loa thing?" asked Jeannine.

"Most likely, if you can believe it," said Curtis.

"I won't even try to understand this supernatural bullshit," she said, standing. "So, let me back up for a moment to more familiar and sane ground."

She turned to Curtis.

"Be honest with me, Curtis. Those bastards who— those men—did you kill them?"

Straight to her case.

"No," said Curtis, head bowed. "I did not kill those men."

"Nah," said Roo. "I found them. It was Charley who'd killed them."

Jeannine looked at Roo for a moment, then stood from her seat on the steps and walked into the living room. "Then why didn't he come forward? Why did he use Curtis's gun?"

"He didn't use my gun," said Curtis. "It must have been planted by the Major. As to why Charley didn't come forward, well . . . "

Roo snorted. "Yeah, the Jewish mythical spirit of revenge, made by a black Baptist soldier, is gonna be a great figure to arrest. I'm sure the cops will be all like 'Yo! You made of clay an' shit? How 'bout you serve ten to twenty in a sandbox? That cool'?"

"Seriously, Roo," said Curtis. "I'm the second whitest guy in this room, next to Gallow, and I'm embarrassed for you when you do that."

"But Roo makes a fair point. I assume Charley is considered dead by the authorities, yes?" asked Jeannine.

"MIA in Iraq," confirmed Gallow.

"He'll be back at dawn tomorrow," said Roo, then corrected himself as he looked at his watch. "Later today, I mean. You can give him the third degree then."

"Okay. That's some more supernatural bullshit that will have to wait," replied Jeannine.

She turned to Curtis once again. "You knew my mother?"

"Yes."

"When did you meet?"

"I knew of her long before I met her. She is a legend—"

"Was," said Jeannine. "I was told she died when I was a teenager. I really don't remember it, though. That's why I was with Nana when . . . when the storm struck."

"You were lied to," said Curtis.

"Seems to be a lot of that going around," said Roo. Fernández and Gallow nodded. Curtis ignored them.

"Before you ask, J, no, I didn't know about Cassandra's fate. Not at first."

"When did you find out?" she asked, her voice barely a whisper.

"Three years after you left for New York," said Curtis. He couldn't look at her.

"Mother-FUCKER!"

"Bernstein called me . . . he told me . . . told me he had made arrangements to keep her locked away for good. And that it was better for you that you never found out, better to think she'd died."

"Stanley . . . He had . . . I'm confused. Wait . . . is she still alive?"

"In a manner of speaking," said Curtis, finally looking at her. "Her body must be alive for her to be able to project her spirit like she does."

"What does that mean?"

"The night Randy and I came to your place . . . the woman who'd been your mother didn't exist anymore. She was . . . deranged. Insane. More animal than anything else. You both were surrounded by piles of human bones. Something . . . "

"Oh God," said Roo. "Something possessed your mother, Jeannine."

"Yeah . . . " said Curtis. His eyes looked beyond Jeannine now, beyond this room, replaying past nightmares. "Possessed. That's what Stanley had said in the call. He told me to leave you alone or there would be . . . consequences."

"Consequences?" Jeannine asked.

"I went and saw her just before Katrina. Your

mother was being held at BCP—the Bayou Cypress Pavilion for the Criminally Insane."

The story was coming fast, now, though Curtis's faraway look intensified.

"She knew me, God only knows how. Knew my name, my wife's name, where I lived. All of it. She even knew of my friends, knew one of them was a golem . . . she knew I'd be leaving the sheriff's department. Of course, I wrote it off . . . ramblings of a crazy woman, or so I thought."

"My mother!" said Jeannine in a voice that demanded silence.

"Yeah, your mother said she was the eleventh Cassandra, I think. Her aunt was the tenth. You would have been the twelfth. Indentured for the Loa to use as it sees fit . . . " Curtis sounded like he was talking in his sleep now. Roo, Gallow, and Fernández all turned to watch him, concerned.

"What . . . what the fuck are you talking about?" spat Jeannine, oblivious of the concern from Curtis's krewe.

"You're right. I'm getting ahead of myself," continued Curtis. "At that point, an orderly in sunglasses came in and told me it was time to leave, that I should forget what I saw. Forget what I heard. It was only later that I learned the orderly was one of Cassandra's minions. An old jazzman called . . . "

"Easy Street," Jeannine finished his sentence for him.

"You know him?" Curtis snapped back from his waking dream.

"I met him. You understand he's dead, right?"

"Yes," said Curtis quietly. "There is something else I need to—"

At that moment, Oliver the cat went mental. The three-legged beast darted around the room hissing and growling.

"Uh-oh," said Roo, looking out the window.

"Cops?" asked Curtis, standing.

"No. My enchantment is holding. That's the good news."

"And the bad news?"

"Perhaps we should have holed up some place that wasn't filled with dead people who are able to apparently ignore my spell work."

Curtis jumped to the window.

"I think Papa Nightmare found us," said Roo. "Should have realized it sooner."

Outside, the raised tombs trembled as marble, cement, and stone cracked and parted—the dead began to crawl toward the caretaker's cottage.

FIFTEEN

Bayou Cypress Pavilion for the Criminally Insane
New Orleans
You are closer to me than any of your predecessors

BCP. She knew this place.

It was once one of the leading state-run psychiatric institutions of the American South. Bayou Cypress Pavilion, better known as BCP, was now a crumbling shell of its former glory. The lobby and east wing were destroyed by the floods of Katrina and a subsequent fire that took a hundred and thirty-seven patients' lives.

Cassandra knew of every death that had occurred due to her storm.

The place had been abandoned during the hurricane, with the most dangerous of inmate patients left to fend for themselves. Locked in their cells, many either chained or sealed in straitjackets, those who didn't drown or burn died from dehydration or starvation. BCP was nearly closed after, with the head administrator given a fine and two years at home with an ankle monitor.

His was the worst punishment handed down to any employee of the facility.

Cassandra mused on these facts, pieced together

from snippets of staff conversations she'd overheard.

No one cared about crazy prisoners—most of whom were black. Cassandra snorted. *If there had been a bunch of Scandinavian-looking inmates at the place, the powers that be would have sent in the Marines.*

What remained of the broken building was scheduled for demolition. But after the storms, there was so much reconstruction work that the skeletal remains of the mental hospital and prison were soon forgotten—as was the injustice of its inmates' demises.

That bit, at least, had been part of Cassandra's plan.

Now, the building couldn't even be seen when driving by. The bayou had reclaimed the wreckage, erasing both the structure and the tragedy from the minds of the locals.

It was as if the building itself had wrapped itself in a protective cloak of trees and moss.

Cassandra's little crumbling castle in the bayou. Crumbling, like she was.

She had been beautiful once. And powerful. Curious, too. And that had led to her biggest failure.

Cassandra liked to push her power to the absolute fringes of possibility. It hadn't been enough for her to perform the ancient rites and spells of her people. Even speaking and raising the dead had lost its luster long ago.

She experimented with powerful psychedelics, along with the blood and powders of her craft. That was when the madness grabbed hold.

That was when she made contact.

BAYOU WHISPERS

Six months before Katrina would devastate the region, she'd heard the whispers from the bayou. A voice had called to her, pleaded with her. Tempted her.

You are closer to me than any of your predecessors. Just a little further. I need your help, my child. I need your love.

That was the Voice, as Cassandra had come to call it. Gentle, like a lover's caress. Firm, like a lover's hand. The Voice had become her constant companion.

The Voice had whispered beautiful things, horrible things. Told her of the past and of her future. Spoke of destiny, of rising again.

You are closer to me than any of your predecessors.

The Voice was asleep, but not asleep. It was imprisoned, just like Cassandra. And only Cassandra could understand the depth of dismay that oozed from every word said to her.

Cassandra didn't know anymore where her thoughts ended, and the Voice began. The Voice, a buzzing that bordered on the orgasmic for the Voudon Queen. Cassandra was as addicted to the pleasure and pain of that Voice as she was to the pharmaceuticals coursing through her veins.

The Voice was jealous, though. During this time, Cassandra had lucid moments—moments where she feared for her sanity, moments where she tried to tell her daughter about the Voice.

The Voice couldn't have that. The girl had potential. The girl might be a threat. Only Cassandra had found favor, found companionship. The bonds with Cassandra's daughter had to be broken, had to be destroyed before the Voice lost its future human host.

It was the Voice, twisting words from soothing to harsh, that convinced Cassandra to kill her daughter.

She tried that very night, with an ancient machete owned by the first Cassandra.

But her daughter had power—so much power. The child, without knowing how, fought off the attack. Undead rose up from the nearby ancient graveyard to take the blows from the old blade—the dead had been called up in a way that frightened Cassandra.

Her daughter was a natural necromancer.

This frightened her because she had no idea how her untrained and undisciplined daughter had done it.

The police were called, and Cassandra, screaming and foaming at the mouth, was hauled away to BCP. For not only had the child protected herself, she had even silenced the Voice.

The child—Jeannine—had been moved that very night to live with Nana. She had no memory of the attack.

For a month, Cassandra lay in her own filth, comatose, in a locked cell chained to a bed.

It took that long for the Voice to find her again.

The reunion snapped Cassandra out of her coma, brought meaning back to her life. The Voice had a sacred task for Cassandra.

The child still needed to die.

The Voice needed Cassandra's help to make that happen. A storm was forming in the Atlantic, one that the Voice could control with Cassandra's help. The Voice was still deep in its slumber—but that could change with the sacrifice of the child and many, many others.

Blood. The Voice needed blood—the human life force would allow the Voice to wake fully, but until then, Cassandra would have to help.

Help me, Dear-heart. You will be rewarded above all others for your service and sacrifice to me. Together we shall return me and my kin to their places of honor.

"How can I serve?" was the first thing Cassandra had said aloud since her incarceration.

The doctors had taken this as a good sign.

The Voice taught Cassandra the words. Provided all the blood she would need for the task. In the end, Katrina was pulled toward New Orleans after its track had taken it into the Gulf.

Cassandra, helped by the Voice, changed the course of a hurricane.

The storm would kill thousands, including Jeannine, all as a gift to Ti Malice.

Those who were left to die in the hospital were given in death to Cassandra. She would need servants for what was to come. The thousands of additional dead went to the Voice. It allowed the sleeping creature to possess Cassandra, destroying the remaining vestiges of the Voudon Queen's identity in the process.

The dead in the hospital eventually made their way to the woman who promised salvation for the troubled souls left behind by the living. She was the light they all gravitated to.

The Voice—the Loa, Ti Malice—welcomed her new servants with open arms.

It will take time, my children. But you will have your revenge. I will wake, and together we will take this world back from those who are trying to destroy it.

But the plan hadn't gone as expected. Jeannine survived yet again, damaged but potentially more dangerous than ever. The Loa would need to gain strength before facing the child again. She would need more blood and she would need to remove the child from her city.

For New Orleans was a city of the damned and dead now. It was Ti Malice's city, the future city of all the Loa.

She needed to get Jeannine LaRue out of the city. Then she would be able to have as much blood as she needed to finally wake—for however long that might take.

SIXTEEN

Greenwood Cemetery Caretaker's Cottage
New Orleans

THEY WERE OUTSIDE the cottage, near the parked truck.

"Roo, can you get to Charley before those things get here?" asked Curtis through gritted teeth.

"Yeah, he's wrapped up—but I hate moving him before the process is complete."

"Get him into the bed of the pickup. Fernández, go with him."

"Do you expect to waltz through a couple hundred zonbi?" asked an incredulous Gallow, as he pulled a shotgun from behind the couch.

"No, I expect we will run away as fast as we can get out of here."

"And go where, Jonesy? My restaurant and house are sure to be covered with cops."

"Back to my place."

"We burned it to the ground, remember?"

"I do. You didn't burn the bunker, though."

"Guys," began Jeannine. "While I appreciate this macho banter, can we move, please? I'm really not interested in hanging out with the dead again, especially if Papa Nightmare is here, too."

An engine roared outside and Roo screamed something unintelligible that Curtis took to mean, "Get your asses in the truck now!"

"Let's move," said Curtis. "Gallow, cover us."

Gallow nodded and fired through the window at the closest rotting corpse crawling toward the cottage.

Curtis grabbed Jeannine and together they ran for Roo's massive pickup.

They never made it.

In seconds, hissing zonbi surrounded Jeannine and Curtis. Curtis looked at Roo, wide-eyed behind the wheel.

"Go!" yelled Curtis to the old man. "150 yards from the trailer toward the creek! Keypad! Georgina's birthday . . . "

Corpses pawed at the truck, leaving Roo with no choice but to stomp on the gas, mangling the living dead as the F-350 tore away from the cemetery.

Jeannine held onto Curtis. But she wasn't afraid, as he'd expected.

She wasn't anything at all.

Her eyes had rolled back into her head and she began to speak in a harsh, guttural voice. She spoke a language that sounded more like the screeching of rats than any known human tongue.

The zonbi halted.

How ever she'd done it, Jeannine had stopped the creatures.

She collapsed in Curtis's arms.

The creatures remained motionless. Shotgun blasts from the cottage died away. Finally, Gallow called out, "Boss?"

But before Curtis could respond, a voice came from behind him.

"My, my, my. Looks like you're in a bit of trouble, Jones."

Curtis knew that voice all too well. He turned to see Randy lighting a cigarette.

"Evenin', partner," was all Curtis replied.

"That was an eighty-thousand-dollar car belongin' to the Major that you destroyed, Jones," said Randy. "That, on top of a wrecked police building and . . . what was that other thing? Oh, yes . . . two dead bayou rats by your own gun. I think it's safe to say you'll be making license plates until the day they stick a needle in your arm."

Randy took a long drag from his cigarette and turned to the cottage. "Gallow! Major says your businesses are safe for now. Appreciate the tip. One of these fine officers will take you home."

He turned back to Curtis with a smile.

"Papa Nightmare's little voodoo tricks are damn useful, ain't they? At least when it's dark. Not so useful in the light of day. Anyway, let's you, me, and the girl go for a ride."

Undisclosed Location

Jeannine didn't know what she was waiting for—all she knew was that she was waiting for . . . something.

She'd drifted in and out of sleep, curled up on the cot, her arms and feet held by the tie wrap things. But her prosthetic must have shifted during her capture—her leg ached. She'd need to take it off soon to catch the swelling before it got so bad she couldn't walk.

I haven't been tied up this much since college.

It had been hours since Randy locked her in here alone. *Had it been hours or minutes?* Time was doing weird things. This cage—that's a word she hadn't used since . . . after Katrina—smelled of cheap cleaner that didn't quite cover the rotting decay and all to human stench of piss and sweat. Dust particles in the air glimmered like tiny insects, given life and purpose by the buzzing, flickering, fluorescent overhead lighting.

The magical rhythm of the lights was soothing, almost hypnotizing: *Buzz, hiss-hiss, flicker. Buzz, hiss-hiss, flicker.*

Something was coming. She knew that much. The feeling—like ice water trickling down her neck to soak her back, her breasts—was something she'd felt before.

It was how she always knew when she was about to be raped.

Whispers, like insects, buzzed around her head. She tried to listen, to make out the words. But they were just out of reach. But the tone sounded mocking, challenging.

If only she could hear the words.

Buzz, hiss-hiss, flicker. Buzz, hiss-hiss, flicker.

"Hello, Jeannine."

The something had arrived.

The air temperature dropped so fast that the sweat on Jeannine's body caused her to shiver. She could turn to look at whatever it was, talk to it as it sat there in the room behind her, but she decided to close her eyes and stay motionless on the cot.

Whatever it was could rot in hell.

"Now, now. Is that anyway to think about your mother?" hissed a voice into her ear.

"My mother . . . or are you Ti Malice? I'm confused," said Jeannine, not moving.

"So, you *do* remember! We had such fun back then."

Jeannine turned her back toward her mother. "You were my everything when I was a little girl. My everything as a teenager. Until you tried to kill me, that is. Just go away, *Mama*. Leave me the fuck alone."

"You did so well, though. Raising the dead as shields. I was so proud of you."

"Is that my mother talking, or the parasite Loa?"

"Both. *We* were so proud."

"Just go away."

"I can't. You need our help."

"I don't want your help," whispered Jeannine, forcing the words out, opening her eyes and noticing for the first time a camera in the top corner of her prison. *I wonder if anyone can see her except me. Is anyone watching? Is anyone listening?* The little red light below the lens was off, so probably not.

"I don't need your help," said Jeannine, correcting herself.

Cassandra laughed. A throaty, rasping sound so sharp it made Jeannine fight the urge to shrink away from such a blade.

A cold hand stroked Jeannine's thigh.

The cell lights continued their monologue:

Buzz, hiss-hiss, flicker. Buzz, hiss-hiss, flicker.

Jeannine focused on a spider near the camera, carefully tending a silken web that wrapped around the warm electronics. *Smart. Catch more food that way.*

She knew Mama/Ti Malice was still there. If she looked, she'd see her: lips peeled back, teeth bared, like a snake about to strike. But she didn't look. She stayed very still, feeling her mother's suffocating presence hovering nearby. Watching the spider spin its web.

"Didn't see us, did you, daughter?" her mother's voice continued. "Didn't see us, watching over you, the way we always have? We, the one shining above. You, the filthy spawn—crawling in the muck of life, dirty hands, dirty mind. Filled with the seed of filthy men."

"Shut up, Cassandra."

"Do you remember what they did? Filthy purple-headed snakes, violating every crease . . . "

"I SAID SHUT YOUR FUCKING MOUTH!"

Buzz, hiss-hiss, flicker. Buzz, hiss-hiss, flicker.

Jeannine finally looked at Cassandra, cot creaking as she turned. But the figure sitting at the foot of the stained cot wasn't the mother she remembered. It was the Cassandra who stood on Nana's shattered roof—her face painted like a skull, hair matted and filthy. The one who had asked her to join with the storm.

The one who had whispered to her for over a decade.

"You should have joined us then, Jeannine," said Cassandra. "If you joined us, we could have been part of the new world about to be born. Now . . . "

Cassandra's hissing breath condensed on Jeannine's skin, and she could almost feel the scrape of sharp teeth against her cheek. Her mother coiled around her.

"Your power is going to taste *so* sweet," whispered her mother.

"Fuck off."

"It's over, Dear-heart. Do you get that? I've won. Soon I will wake. Soon my brothers and sisters will wake. And we will remake the world the way it was, before the filth of humanity stained it. There is nothing you can do to prevent our plan."

Cassandra lay down next to Jeannine on the narrow cot, sliding so close Jeannine didn't know where she began, and the Loa ended.

"I grow stronger with each death," said Cassandra. "Each drop of blood brings me closer to wakefulness. Let me help you out of this place. Then you can join me. I offer this gift to you one last time."

In her mind, Jeannine floated above the two of them. She saw herself practically spooning with her mother on the cot. But then, Cassandra's mouth opened wide—wider than it should have been able, dislocating like a snake eating a particularly large meal. Jeannine felt herself falling into a chasm of teeth, saliva surrounded by fetid breath . . .

The metal door to her cage opened with a loud creak and Jeannine shook herself awake.

Randy stood there with a plastic tray holding a hot sandwich on a plate along with a cup of steaming coffee.

"I thought you might be hungry," he said. "The only thing you've eaten in the last twenty-four hours has been airline food."

Jeannine wasn't going to touch the food—a small act of defiance. But the coffee smelled so good. Less than a minute later, she was sipping fresh hot coffee while Randy pulled a metal chair into her cell.

"The guards heard voices in here," he said. "But the damn camera is offline . . . "

"I was having a fabulous sex dream," replied Jeannine.

"With someone named Cassandra?"

"Tut. It takes all kinds. Plus, it doubles my chance for a date Saturday night."

Randy's mouth twitched once. "Why were you dreaming of your mother?"

"I don't put any stock into dreams," replied Jeannine. "Why are you holding me?" The coffee helped the Ice Queen get back some of her mojo. "Can you please tell me what I've done wrong, other than to consult with my client about his case? Speaking of which, where *is* my client?"

Randy shrugged slowly, ignoring her questions. "For all I know, you helped him escape and were harboring a fugitive."

"I was on a plane! Ask your Major, he was kind enough to meet me at the airport."

"True. But until we can prove that, we have the right to hold you."

"And I have the right to counsel, which I'm invoking right now."

"You are assuming you're in a police facility of some sort. You're not. The Major has . . . other detention places he likes to use when necessary."

"Lawyer. Now, motherfucker."

"Suit yourself," said Randy, standing. "Boys! Take her to the sheriff's station. Let the Major deal with her. Take Jones outside, I'll put a bullet in his pretty head myself."

"A bullet in your pretty head."

"No," screamed a voice in Jeannine's head. "I'll do whatever you want! Don't kill me!"

The two men laughed as they stared down at her. One wore a filthy, stained John Deere ball cap and had teeth as black as coal; the other with hair and a beard so long, matted, and tangled. They looked as if they'd never seen either soap or a comb.

"We thought you'd be seeing things our way," said ball cap, putting his large handgun back into his waistband. "I get to go first," he said to his compatriot.

"How come you get to go first?" asked the long-haired man. "I saw her first . . . hangin' onto that roof, lookin' so pretty . . . "

"'Cause I got the gun, retard, that's why."

"I got me a big knife, though," said matted beard.

"Well, I got no problem doin' it at the same time. Which hole you want first?"

Jeannine felt helpless, powerless. She began to cry.

"Keep that up and I'll put a bullet in yo' head myself," said ball cap. "You will like everything we do to you. And you will ask us for more. You'll smile as we fuck you again and again and again and . . . "

"Cassandra," hissed Jeannine, snapping back to the present. She stared at Randy, on his feet in front of her, hand on his gun. The bastard was so eager to carry out Curtis's execution.

"I accept your offer," she said.

The air in the cage suddenly felt heavy and the temperature once again plunged.

"Just like your mother, ain't you," said Randy, shaking his head. "You're one slice shy of a grilled cheese sandwich, lady."

"Perhaps. But my mother is here, and she really doesn't like you very much."

"You need help, sweetheart . . . "

"Help? Oh . . . help is a good idea. And I'll get

some. But you're gonna need some, too. The sad part is you don't realize it yet."

Jeannine laughed. Or maybe she cried. She couldn't tell the difference anymore. *What have I done?* She was still laughing when the two burly cops shackled her again, and when they helped her to her feet and marched her out of the cage.

"She's still here," Jeannine called out to Randy. Not that she thought he'd listen. "Cassandra's the one you want to speak to. But she's always hungry."

No one was listening. No one believed her. Typical men.

"Bye, Mama," she whispered as she left the room. "I'll see you soon."

⚜

The cell was empty now. Randy stood alone inside it. In the hall, the guards ordered Jeannine to walk. Their footsteps made it down a dirty, flooded hallway, and then the distant clang of the door closing and locking behind them.

"All right, Curtis. Your turn," muttered Randy, standing.

The Major said after this one favor, they'd be square. One little indiscretion, and the Major's held it over me ever since.

The sooner I can finish this job, the better.

Buzz, hiss-hiss, flicker. Buzz, hiss-hiss, flicker.

Creeeeek.

He turned and looked at the cot.

For a moment, Randy felt like he was a small child in his bedroom after the light was turned off, tucking his hands in tight beneath the blankets so the monsters couldn't find him. He hesitated, his heart pounding strangely fast in his chest, then bent down to look under the cot.

Nothing.

Of course, there was nothing.

Shaking his head, he got to his feet. Not enough sleep this week. Or last week. It was definitely getting to him. He turned to leave, when he heard a faint scraping of metal on concrete.

The door.

And on the edge of the door, strangely elongated, thin shadows curved around the edges, like clawed fingers or talons grasping at the wood.

A hiss—a ragged breath.

Buzz, hiss-hiss, flicker. Buzz, hiss-hiss, flicker.

Laughter, like a teenage girl's giggle. Then music.

It was just one of those things
Just one of those crazy flings
One of those bells that now and then rings
Just one of those things.

The door closed. The lock clicked.

The lights went out.

"She's not your sweetheart," gurgled a child-like voice.

Randy never even had time to scream.

SEVENTEEN

Undisclosed Location

CURTIS AWOKE IN some sort of cell. The dampness reminded him of the hole in the ground he had been kept in for a week in Columbia.

He shook his head, the cobwebs faded, and his mind cleared. He had a vague recollection of Roo's place, bodies crawling toward him. Shotgun blasts . . .

Gallow. That fucking traitor. He always was a political pussy, cutting deals to save his own skin. That's why Curtis had ended up in that hole in the ground in Columbia, too. It all made sense now. Gallow's restaurant in the French Quarter was never a place where he wanted the krewe to meet. "Bad for business, having you criminals around," Gallow had always said.

But crooked cops with the entire state in their pocket?

Well, that would ensure Gallow's place of power within the corrupt local government.

How did Curtis never see it?

Gallow had saved Curtis's life during the war. But because Gallow's motivations were always so coated with self-interest, he'd been the last one asked to join the krewe. Charley hadn't cared—being dead could be like that. But Fernández and Roo had voiced their concerns over Gallow's connections and political aspirations.

And he, Curtis, had overridden those concerns. After all, the man had saved him.

"Dumbass," he admonished himself. His voice sounded dull, just like when he'd been held underground in Columbia.

He heard laughter. Then screaming outside his door.

The silence returned as suddenly as the screaming had started.

The door to his cell opened.

Jeannine stood there, covered in blood.

Just like before.

Toulouse Street
French Quarter, New Orleans
February 2005

"Tell me again why the Major loaned us out to the 8th district commander?" asked Officer Curtis Jones, as he blew smoke out the passenger side window of his patrol car. Despite the winter chill, the music blared in the streets, and the people sang, walking from bar to bar, arm in arm, laughing and enjoying the spectacle that was Bourbon Street.

This time of year, the temperature in the city was cold enough to elicit a shiver from those whose blood had thinned because of the long hot summers—or the vast quantities of alcohol served every twenty feet or so. Even with the heater at full blast, and the window only opened a crack to let out his cigarette smoke, Jones and his partner Randy wore gloves and overcoats to combat the cold.

It was as if winter had claimed New Orleans and refused to let go.

"Parish departmental collaboration," said Randy, a cigarette hanging from his mouth, a half inch of ash defying gravity.

Both men sucked on their non-filtered Camels at the same moment, twin red flares lighting the interior of their patrol car.

"And why do we have to wear their damn uniforms?" grumbled Jones.

"Because powder blue is your color, *mon ami*," replied Randy.

"Fuck you," said Curtis.

"Dispatch to car twenty-eight," crackled a voice over the radio.

"Jesus, why is that so loud?" growled Jones as he picked up the mic.

"Twenty-eight. Go, Dispatch."

"A 103-D reported at 1043 Toulouse Street at the corner of Rampart. You country boys need directions?"

"Twenty-eight is good, thanks, Dispatch. On our way. Out." Jones clicked off the mic and added, "Bitch."

"Disturbance, huh?" said Randy. "You never know, Jonesy. We might get lucky and find a crazy guy with a knife."

"We're not that lucky," said Jones. "Hit the lights and siren, will ya? I want to scare some of these tourists out of our way."

BAYOU WHISPERS

They left the brightly lit and colorful part of town, with its music and laughter, and turned onto a quiet street bathed in greys and browns. Here, cracked sidewalks and garbage were left unfixed and uncleaned, respectively. Tourists didn't come around here often enough for the streets to warrant the city's attention.

They pulled up to a typical Creole townhouse, a three-story solid brick building with cast-iron balconies. The mortar work was dilapidated. Fallen bricks lay on the overgrown foot path outside the home and dark streaks adorned the front door. Jones could make out little else, as there were no lights on at the place.

In fact, the entire block was dark.

"I don't like this, Randy. Feels really wrong," said Jones.

"You wanna deal with the Major when he finds out we called in backup for a simple disturbance? Get a hold of yourself, Jonesy." But despite his words, Randy unclipped the strap to free up the sidearm on his belt as he got out of the car. He flipped the safety off, too.

Jones did the same.

Randy took a couple of steps, slipping on some sort of muck. "What the hell is all this mud doing on the sidewalk?" whispered Randy—the only sound in the stillness of a winter night. No dogs barked. No music played. There were no signs of life at all.

"Looks like someone dug up a garden. Maybe that was the disturbance? And what's that smell? Smells like an open latrine," said Jones, matching Randy's whisper.

"I don't smell nothin'," said Randy.

Carefully, each with one hand on their gun and the other holding a Maglite, the officers approached the front door of the townhouse. Under the scan of his flashlight, Jones realized that the door decolorization was caused by mud splashed on the faded and peeling wood.

The door was ajar.

"Fuck, this really feels wrong, Randy. I'll take the heat," said Jones as he went to speak into the shoulder mic attached to his portable radio.

"No way!" hissed Randy and he pushed open the front door. "Police!" he called. "We're coming in!"

Laughter.

"That sounded like a little girl," said Jones.

"That sounded creepy as all fuck," said Randy. "Standard sweep. Cover me. We do not get separated."

They quickly cleared the first floor and returned to the staircase. Randy called out again, "Police! Is anyone here?"

More laughter.

"Maybe we should wait for backup," said Curtis.

"Someone might be hurt," said Randy.

"Malice-malice-malice-malice," chanted a singsong voice.

"There's mud on the stairs," said Jones. He knew his partner already thought he was weak. Time to remind Randy that he was an ex-Army Ranger. "I'm heading up. Cover me."

Jones climbed the stairs, nearly slipping once on the mud. The gelatinous mess became thicker the higher they climbed. The muttering grew louder as they reached the top of the stairs. A woman's voice, saying one word over and over.

"Malice."

Jones silently pointed at the second door on the left. Randy nodded.

They crept across the mud-caked carpet.

Randy stumbled. He and Jones instinctively swung their Maglite's toward the ground.

It was a femur. A human femur on the floor. With a large gash in the center of the bone.

"Malice-malice-malice-malice . . . "

They burst into the room where the voice came from—to find a scene right out of hell itself.

A young girl, maybe fourteen, sat on the bed. She was covered in blood and mud, her brown eyes wide and unblinking.

Surrounding her on the bed and floor were piles of bones that looked as though they'd been hacked apart. Mud caked everywhere.

A woman sat cross-legged among the bones at the foot of the bed. She rocked back and forth, giggling and muttering— "malice-malice-malice."

She held a machete and cut her forearm: one dark red line each time she spoke the word.

"Malice-malice-malice."

Dark red droplets pooled around her.

Randy and Jones pointed their pistols and screamed at her to drop the weapon.

The woman laughed and continued to mutter, drool oozing down one side of her mouth.

"Don't worry," said the girl on the bed in a detached, calm voice. "She can't hurt you now. I have her mind."

"Malice-malice-malice-malice . . . "

139

Undisclosed Location

"Jeannine, are you all right?" asked Curtis, sitting up in his cot with a creak of rusted springs. "What happened?"

"Time to go, Curtis," she said in a detached, calm voice.

"Go? Go where?" he asked.

"We're going to pay my mother a visit," replied Jeannine. "I'm tired of speaking with her spirit. It's time for us to speak to the flesh and blood Cassandra."

Though she spoke forcefully, Jeannine stood still as a statue. He'd seen her like this before, of course. Once. After her mother tried to kill her.

"Why are we going to see her, J?"

"Because I need to cut off her head," said Jeannine with no affect at all.

EIGHTEEN

The Sultana

EASY STREET HAD always loved playing his horn. The music naturally flowed from him. His mama had never been able to afford him lessons when he was younger.

When he was alive.

He'd stolen his sax—Ms. Maxine, as he'd lovingly named her—from a white man who owned a pawn shop long since bulldozed. Old man Gene loved to beat on black people, especially children. Nobody cared back then. Mostly, they still didn't care, from what Easy Street had seen.

So, he stole Ms. Maxine. But try as he might, he couldn't get a sound out of her.

Until a man named Reggie explained what a "reed" was and taught him how to blow into the horn all proper. He even taught the boy how to hold the instrument. Reggie played records for him, and young Easy Street listened, then noodled on the horn until he found the right notes. In less than a month, the kid was able to play old Ms. Maxine like a pro.

"Boy," said Reggie one day, "I never heard nor done seen the like. You is a natural, you is. From now on you be on Easy Street."

And, thus, his stage name was born.

He was nine years old.

It was some years after when Papa Nightmare had used him in a game that the old Bokor knew the late jazzman would lose.

If only the old jazzman knew then what he knew now.

Yes, ole' Easy had been set up by Cassandra and his bandmate Fat Freddie. But Fat Freddie met his own demise, lying in a flop house, covered in shit and piss. Easy had made sure his corpse lay rotting in filth that whole summer. Served him right for putting two bullets in Easy's head.

These thoughts were happening as Easy's fingers caressed Ms. Maxine, while he blew out a melancholy tune for the thousandth time aboard the *Sultana*.

He used just the right amount of vibrato to make the women weep.

Papa Nightmare. The jazzman sighed and continued to play.

Oh, how he wished the spell binding him was something a poor jazzman could break. He'd pleaded with Cassandra to take him back, but she'd laughed and told him that Papa Nightmare wanted to keep his court jester, and that she'd have no use for a dead musician. He was a ghoul with no purpose, damned to entertain dead soldiers, being laughed at while that bastard Bokor thought up new ways to torture him.

"Hello, Easy Street. Ms. Maxine."

The female voice came from behind. Easy slowly took the sax out of his mouth. *What new torture is this?*

"It's not torture, I assure you. I want to have a chat," said the woman's voice.

"He knows you're here, little *plaçage*. He will come for you," replied Easy.

"Papa Nightmare?" The voice behind him laughed. "He is too busy licking Ti Malice's devil button at the moment, falsely secure in thinking his beloved ship is untouchable. Which is why I've come to see you."

This was not the angry lawyer lady from New York. This was . . . something else.

Easy turned to Jeannine. She was there, but not there. A projection.

He smiled.

"You've cut a deal," he said simply.

"I have," she confirmed.

"My, my, my. The little scared *plaçage* is learning all sorts of new things, isn't she? I dig it."

"You keep calling me that. My French is . . . non-existent. What does it mean?"

"Mixed race," said Easy. "It's what people with a similar . . . affliction . . . were called back in the day. Among other things."

"Ah. You mean it as an insult. Does the fact that my mother is black, and my father is white concern you?"

"Not at all, Ms. Jeannine. I merely point out a fact of your birth prompted by your question of me."

"I never knew my father. And my mother? Well, she is a piece of work, that's for sure."

"Your mother is the niece of a whore," spat Easy. The memory was painful, which is why Papa Nightmare used it to torture the sax player.

"Be careful, motherfucker. I'm here as your potential savior."

"Oh? Do tell."

"I have a simple task for you. Two, actually."

"I am a servant to Papa Nightmare. You cannot order me or even ask me to do anything without his knowledge, *plaçage*."

"Since you insist on calling me *plaçage*. Can I call you 'slave,' then?"

Easy's lips tightened, disappearing into a fine line.

"Ah, I see the term infuriates you—as it should," Jeannine continued. "Shall we stop with the nonsense? I have made a deal with Cassandra that has given me a certain . . . power. And knowledge."

Jeannine's image moved toward Easy Street. She stroked the worn leather lip of Ms. Maxine's case. The case glowed.

"Carry Ms. Maxine with you and your thoughts shall be your own around Papa Nightmare," said Jeannine. "Do you trust me?" she asked, looking up at Easy Street.

"Not at all, little *pla* . . . Ms. Jeannine."

She smiled. "Acceptable. Will you perform a couple simple tasks for me?"

"Depends on what they is," said Easy warily.

"After I deal with my mother in her hospital lair, you will capture me and bring me to this boat and present me to Papa Nightmare."

Easy grinned. "That will curry me favor with Papa Nightmare and place you again in harm's way. I can do that, no problem."

"Ah, but you haven't heard my other request."

"Pray, do tell."

"I need you to retrieve something of my mother's. I have no idea where it may be, but you will find it and place it where I tell you."

Easy cocked his head, curious.

"Do these things for me, and I will be able to release you from Papa Nightmare's spell," said Jeannine. "Do you agree?"

She watched the emotions play across Easy's face. Even with the dark glasses, she could tell he was thinking it over. *Was she full of shit? Could she actually free him? Would she be a better master?*

She saw his answer even before he said it aloud.

"What do you want me to get for you?" he asked.

Undisclosed Location

"Jeannine?" asked Curtis for the third time.

"We have to go. She knows we are coming," said Jeannine in that flat tone.

"Why are you covered in blood? What happened?"

"We have the help of a new ally now. But we have to go," she repeated. She turned on her heel and walked down the hallway.

Curtis got off his cot and followed her. In a hallway of cinder blocks with one hanging lightbulb, he felt trapped in a scene from an '80s slasher film. Blood and internal organs splattered the floor, walls, and ceiling. A few red drops smoked slightly on the single bulb that swung lazily from the ceiling.

The enclosed space smelled of offal and death. Curtis gagged.

"Jesus Christ! Jeannine . . . what . . . what did you do?"

"They were going to kill us and bury us out back in graves that had already been dug," she answered.

"Their bones begged me for freedom. So, I granted their wish. They will help us now."

Covering his nose, Curtis made his way behind Jeannine. His feet made squishing sounds against the entrails as they walked down the hall toward a set of cement steps. A pair of metal Bilco doors at the top of the stairs were already open. Jeannine and Curtis climbed up and, upon surfacing, found a St. Dismas Parish police SUV parked nearby. Curtis glanced beyond the bunker and saw two open, unmarked holes unmistakably meant as graves.

How did she know?

Two figures stood at attention by the police SUV. Curtis stopped dead.

In that moment, he remembered his favorite boyhood movie was *Jason and the Argonauts*—the old Ray Harryhausen stop-motion animation classic. He must have watched that movie a hundred times—and every time for the same reason.

He liked the animated skeletons.

As a boy, he always wanted an army of them for himself.

"Mary, Mother of God," he said.

"I will need you to drive. I don't think they can, nor can I, in my current state," said the blood-soaked woman beside him.

"What the hell happened, Jeannine?" asked Curtis.

"Later. And you will call me Cassandra, now."

NINETEEN

U-Store-It!
Public Self-Storage Units off of Interstate 12

FERNÁNDEZ KEPT TRYING Curtis's burner. Gallow's, too. They rang out.

"Still not picking up," he said.

"Something's obviously happened," said Roo. "We'll lay low at my cousin's storage place until we hear from them."

"Why a storage place?" asked Fernández.

"It's one of my bolt holes," said Roo. "I have a pass card that gives me twenty-four-hour access."

He turned his truck into the facility, stopping at the gate long enough to buzz himself in. He saw the security cameras but was nonplused about hiding from them. Beside him, Fernández struggled to hide his face.

"The place belongs to my cousin," said Roo. "I got him out of trouble a while back. He lets me use one of the bigger units here as payment. His boys will erase the camera footage as soon as they come in later this morning."

Fernández relaxed a little. "Who else knows about this place?"

"Jonesy does. He'll figure we're laying low and

he'll show when he and Gallow finish up. Trust me, it's safe here. Besides, we have a clay body in the back we need to reanimate at dawn. You suggesting we do that at Gallow's restaurant? Perhaps as he serves up some eggs Benedict?"

"Fair point," conceded Fernández.

"It's not a bad place to hide for a while. We're backed up to a branch of the Old Mississippi here. The cops'll have to come from the road, so we'll know when they're comin'. We'll be okay here. You'll see."

"One way in means only one way out," countered Fernández. "Which means we'll have to go through whoever comes for us."

"Nah. We'll be okay until we get the Golem back."

"Besides Jonesy, who else might know we're here?"

"Just my cousin Tyrone and you," replied Roo. "I guess I'll have to kill you later," he snorted.

"Not funny, Roo."

"Lighten up, *hombre*. We've been in worse scrapes."

Fernández gaped at Roo in shocked disbelief. "The fuck we have," he muttered.

"Fallujah. Bogotá. Islamabad," Roo counted off. "Want me to go on?"

"I don't remember no zombie corpses crawling after us in Islamabad," sulked Fernández.

"That opioid cartel. Those guys were high as fuck. Same thing."

Fernández grunted.

Roo's F-350 rumbled past a row of closed, brightly painted doors and made its way toward the back of the property. Roo got out of the cab, unlocked a large brass padlock, and rolled up the garage door. He pulled the truck in, stopped the engine, and closed the door from the inside.

"Hey!" Fernández called out in the pitch blackness.

"Hang on, midget!" returned Roo. He swore as his shin banged off something heavy, then his fingers found the light switches.

Large work lights lit a room that was easily 1,500-square-feet in size. Fernández whistled.

"You have a lot of shit, bro," he called.

"Eh?" said Roo, cupping a hand to his ear. "I'm deaf, man, remember? You weren't just whining about something, were you?"

There was a soft thump and an air handler kicked in. The room cooled quickly, and the remaining smells of the river just a dozen yards away and the diesel from the F-350 faded.

"There's a set of cots against the back wall," called Roo. "Make yourself at home."

Fernández found two Army surplus cots separated by a milk crate with a lamp set on it. A paperback book lay open, spine up, on the makeshift nightstand. Fernández made himself comfortable on the cot and picked up the book.

"Holy shit, man. You read romance novels?"

"Mind your business, midget," groused Roo, as he walked over carrying a large case. "Remember, you're only a guest here."

The more Fernández looked around Roo's hideout, the more impressed he became with his friend's preparedness. He whistled, and said, "You could live in here for weeks, *hombre*."

"Months," corrected Roo, as he placed the large case on the empty cot and then opened it.

Fernández whistled again. "That's some pretty heavy-duty hardware, man."

"What good is a bolt hole if you can't protect it? You try calling Curtis again?"

"Yeah, still nothing. Gallow's not picking up, either."

Fernández tossed the cell on a box and began to pace.

Roo sat heavily on his cot. "So, wanna talk about it?"

"Nope."

"C'mon, *hombre*," replied Roo. "That's twice we were attacked by the undead. It's all getting worse. I know it. *You* know it."

"So, by me saying I didn't want to talk about it . . . "

" . . . means that I can do all the talking, so unless you've changed your fucking mind, shut your pie hole while I try and work this out."

"We faced the same thing in Columbia," shrugged Fernández.

"And we lost Sanchez, Fitz, and that Greek kid . . . "

"Theopolous," supplied Fernández.

"Yeah. He was a good kid."

"They were *all* good kids, Roo. What's bothering you about this particular shit-storm?"

"We've been kept off balance for months. The Major snapping at our heels, finally arresting Jonesy. Papa Nightmare's businesses turning more and more violent. The bodies are piling up."

"That tends to happen when we're involved," said Fernández.

"Yeah," said Roo, standing and pacing. "That's my goddamn point. We used to be in control of these things. We never killed anyone, unless they were—"

"*Muy mal.* Yes, I know."

"And never women or children, right? Always bad guys and always when it was a "them or us" situation."

"So?"

"In the last twenty-four hours, we blasted a 27-ton truck through police HQ, Curtis threatened to shoot *some cops*, and we've been assaulted by a couple score of undead."

"Thanks for summing it up for me," snorted Fernández. "I was there for most of it."

"It smells funny, is all. When we torched Curtis's place a few hours ago, I grabbed a notebook I saw in one of his AC vents."

"Roo . . ."

"It's in the truck. I usually don't pry, but shit hasn't been this weird around here since Katrina. Since Jeannine and Curtis were both here. And as soon as she hits the ground here, all hell breaks loose again."

"You're blaming the girl? For fuck's sake, man."

Roo dropped heavily back down on his cot. "Yeah, yeah. I know. Crazy talk. But there's something not right—with Curtis."

"He hasn't been the same since he lost Georgina, man. And he's getting framed for a double murder we both know he didn't commit, since the guy who did is currently a clay statue in the back of your truck."

"Okay, I'm just tired, ya know? That armored car heist would have set us all up for life. Gallow was right—Curtis screwed us over. And I just want to be done with all this bullshit."

Fernández moved over to sit next to Roo on the cot. He put a hand on the older man's shoulder. "We ain't done yet, man. Rangers lead the way."

Roo nodded. "Rangers lead the way."

"You got anything to drink around here?"

"There's a full-sized fridge next to your cot," said Roo. "Grab yourself a beer and toss me one while you're at it. It's gonna be a long night. Might as well be comfortable."

"What about a latrine?" asked Fernández, as he tossed a Coors Light to Roo.

"Five-gallon tub near the big doors. A stack of TP nearby—and a can of Lysol, you smelly bastard."

"For fuck's sake, it was *one* time . . . "

"The fucking place was condemned, *hombre.*"

"*Pendejo. Tu madre huele.* You sure nobody knows about this place?" asked Fernández.

"I told you: just the boss, you, Gallow, and my cousin. And he's as loyal as you and Jonesy. We're safe until we hear from him or Gallow. I just wish dawn would hurry up. I'd like to have the Golem watching our back. And I wish Jonesy and Gallow were here, too."

Louisiana State Trooper Headquarters
Baton Rouge
Operations Command Center

The tech was reviewing video footage from multiple sources. He was running an algorithm based on the description of the truck and tag numbers.

One of his many computers beeped, then zoomed in on a grainy image.

The computer beeped twice more.

"Watch commander, I think you should see this."

An older officer sporting a perfectly pressed uniform and a buzz cut walked over to the young man. The officer held a mug of untouched black coffee. The stencil on the outside of the mug read, "Shut Da Fuh Cup."

"What is it, deputy?" growled the older man.

The young man swallowed. "Uh, we got a hit on that truck Major Dufresne of the St. Dismas Sheriff's Office is lookin' for."

"Let me see, boy," said the watch commander, as he leaned in. "And if you're wrong . . . "

The younger state trooper swung back to his computer and rapidly punched a few keys, a bead of sweat appearing on his brow. The young man played the compiled video feed he'd been sent.

"This first one is from a series of traffic cams leaving N'orleans and crossing north over the Lake Pontchartrain Causeway," he said. He let the scene switch a couple of times, zooming in on the last angle to show the bed of the truck and the vehicle's tag.

"The tag matches," said the watch commander. "But what is that wrapped up in the bed? Is that a . . . body?"

"Dunno, sir," said the trooper. "Looks that way, but no way to tell from these clips."

"All right. Continue."

"After that I lost it for a while, but in scanning the feeds, I found this. It's from an ATM machine at a bank across the street from a U-Store-It! facility on I-12 outside of Lacombe."

On the pixilated black and white video, an old Ford pickup pulled into the self-storage lot.

"Freeze and zoom," barked the watch commander. The video froze. They zoomed in on the license plate. It was grainy, but the commander made out the first three characters.

They matched.

"That's them, all right. Good job, son. I'll call Major Dufresne."

TWENTY

Bayou Cypress Pavilion for the Criminally Insane
New Orleans

THE BAYOU CALLED to her with scents and sounds—wrapping around her like a favorite blanket. She smelled glorious stagnant pools filled with muck and slime; the subtle peaty smell of decaying leaves and wood—the beautiful, fetid scent of animal flesh giving back to the insects and the plants and the waters of the bayou. Nocturnal animals called for their mates, ate one another, raised their young, and fought over territory. Massive birds screamed at the reptiles trying to hide their hunger.

The bayou whispered her new name, whispered approval at her plan.

But someone else controlled her body, controlled her thoughts. She fought against it, but the struggle took all her strength. The power of the Loa was as frightening as the knowledge that flooded into her. The bayou laughed at her.

Ti Malice laughed at her.

This is just a taste, child. It's your turn now.

For Jeannine knew, now, that Cassandra and Ti Malice were one and the same. While the Loa slept deep in the bayou, a small piece of its consciousness had woken and learned to work through a human host. Her mother was truly gone. Jeannine tried to hold on to the memories of the good times—before the attack.

Before Katrina.

Jeannine's mind was filling with the knowledge she needed to be of service. To be the Loa's slave. She hated that word and all that came with it.

Jeannine knew a lot of things now. But the little pocket of her mind that was still hers—still hidden from Cassandra, from Ti Malice—was still an intelligent person, still a lawyer. And the lawyer pieced together even more information to build a case of sorts.

And a plan.

It would be risky. She might die. But death would be welcome if she couldn't end the excruciating pain of the struggle. Since Katrina, she had struggled. Every day. Until now, she'd always thought the struggle was a byproduct of the rapes and torture. But she knew now that she struggled against something far worse—a darkness that wanted to consume her, feed her very soul to Cassandra like the corpses of the creatures feeding the bayou itself.

Key to her fully embracing the role of Cassandra was acceptance of the Loa's power by her own free will. She *knew* that. She also knew that to completely transform into the next Cassandra, "Jeannine"—the essence of her being—had to die. That last part was what she'd been struggling with since Katrina and the aftermath—and especially now. She had to hold onto as much of "Jeannine" as she could.

There might not be a better time to break the cycle than now. When her mother had begun to transfer power to her back in the cell, Jeannine had felt her strength building while her mother grew weaker.

Without a vessel to work through, Ti Malice would . . .

Would . . .

"Stop the vehicle, Curtis," she heard her voice say. She knew what Cassandra had done to the cops—the skeletal escorts whose bones still dripped blood and were held together with magic blacker than night. She knew what the "Cassandra" within her had planned for her mother. And Papa Nightmare.

Jeannine now had a plan, too. But she didn't know if she had the strength to stop the Loa, let alone its minions: Papa Nightmare. The Major. Stanley.

Oh, God, where is Stanley?

She hated him. And loved him. He used her. He saved her.

Every thought was a jumble now in her emotions. All of her struggling against the immense power that was Cassandra.

Jeannine felt her body turn toward the bone soldiers in the back.

"You two," she said. "Clear us a path to the ruins. Do it now."

The undead silently opened the back doors and crawled to the edge of the bayou overgrowth. The creatures began to rip at the grasses and small briars that impeded the path to the shattered building.

"Now what?" asked Curtis, watching from the driver's seat as the undead attacked the bayou. It was the first thing he'd said since they'd escaped the Major's prison.

"Now, Dear-heart," replied Jeannine from beside him. "We shall have a chat with my moth—ugh!"

Jeannine's body convulsed, her ice-blue eyes rolled back in her head and she began to foam at the mouth.

"Jeannine!" Curtis reached over and tried to undo her seatbelt, but she was thrashing so much, he couldn't get to the buckle.

Jeannine lost control of her body, muscles contracting and relaxing randomly as she struggled with Cassandra's attack on her mind. Her mother chased her through her memories, changing images from the past to use as weapons to destroy her identity.

Jeannine needed to change her tactics in this war—or her very soul would be lost.

Nowhere

"Hello, Dear-heart," said the voice.

"What do you want, Mother?" replied Jeannine.

The two women faced each other in a dark place. A place with no depth and no light. A place that stretched to the infinite in all directions. Yet, even though this place was devoid of light, they saw each other clearly.

Both wore pure white Haitian karabela dresses—an off-the-shoulder bodice with a full, matching skirt made of heavy fabric with lace and ricrack—along with matching head scarves.

Jeannine's mother's ice-blue eyes bore into her own.

"Why do you resist so, my daughter?" asked Cassandra. "This is natural—the passing of Cassandra from mother to daughter. It's an honor to be the human vessel for Ti Malice. My time comes to an end. This is your time now and we welcome you, child, with open arms. Yet, you fight us. Why?"

"Unlike you, I don't want this. I don't want to *serve* some sort of creature hell-bent on destroying the world."

"Not destroying, Dear-heart. Saving it."

"Really, Mama? You sound like a cartoon villain. If this place had a chair, I'd sit while you told me the Loa's evil plan."

"The Loa aren't evil, child. Nor are they good. They just are. They were content to sleep while the old gods dispersed, leaving humanity as caretakers of this place. They provided us with a garden, a paradise. Now look what man hath wrought."

"Wait," said Jeannine, confused. "Are you saying Ti Malice wants to save the whales? Stop deforestation?"

"Is it so wrong to live in harmony with the beasts and the trees?"

"No, but killing everyone is not a good thing, Mama."

"Why not? If we don't stop, we will kill ourselves off anyway—and take the planet with us. Ti Malice likes this world. She would rather kill you all and 'save the whales' as you put it."

"Mama, I've accepted your deal. I'm connected to this Loa thing. I *know* what its true intentions are. And it has nothing to do with saving the planet. When the blood it feeds on from humans stops flowing, where will it get its blood from? How will it feed itself then?"

"That is not *our* concern, Dear-heart. Our role is to wake Ti Malice once and for all."

"Well, I'm going to stop it and stop you."

Cassandra laughed.

"I am stronger than Papa Nightmare," she hissed. "I can show you things that will break your stubborn mind. To bring you over to our side. To make you *yearn* for Ti Malice's love like I once loved you, my daughter."

"Mama, I've lived and survived horrors beyond most people's worst fears."

"But unlike Papa Nightmare, who at the end of the day is but a man, I know, as your mother, what frightens you most."

"Being gang raped as a teenager for two months straight wasn't frightening enough?"

"You are of two races, of two peoples, of two worlds. Yet, you yearn for the privileged white world Stanley Bernstein has molded you for. Do you know who you are? Who you *truly* are, my daughter?"

"There are plenty of people like me," said Jeannine. The question bothered her more than she wanted to let on.

"There is no one like you, child. Remember when you were a little girl? Before life became so complicated?"

A little girl in bed. Her mother reading stories to her while she nestled in her mother's arms. Singing hymns in church, voices sounding like angels, praising God's name. A trip to the aquarium, walking in a glass tunnel surrounded by the sea. Such wonders . . .

"Such fun we had! Remember? I can show you nightmares, too," continued her mother.

"I made peace with my nightmare, Mama."

"Really? Let us see."

BAYOU WHISPERS

Two young women walked out from behind Cassandra. One black and one white. They, too, had ice-blue eyes and were clothed in all white Haitian dresses.

"Behold, your eternal struggle," said Cassandra.

Both women were Jeannine. One black and one white. The same but different. Jeannine watched as the black version of herself swirled and warped.

Suddenly, she is back in New York, in college. Furious that a white girl won the RA scholarship, despite the fact she was more qualified. She watches the black version of herself make love to a white man only to be told that he wanted to try some "dark meat." A bar filled with white people jeer at her, call her "nigger," and a bottle is thrown at her, cutting her face. A fat white guy with a comb-over says her "type" isn't right for the company. A black man punches her, calls her a "whore," then stabs her belly with a knife, carving out her uterus killing the child within.

Suddenly, the vision starts again, but it's different this time. She is back in New York, winning a spot on the cheerleading squad, beating out all the women of color, laughing at their disappointed looks. She watches herself make money fucking black guys for films, driving a fancy car. She sees herself throw a bottle at a black woman in a bar; the woman, staggered by the blow, bleeds from a gash in her scalp. A white man punches her, calls her a "whore," then stabs her belly with a knife, carving out her uterus, killing the child within.

"STOP."

Jeannine breathed heavily, her dress soaked in sweat, one hand holding her lower abdomen. "Is this the nightmare you chose for me, Mama? A series of clichéd racial stories ending in a metaphor for how powerless women are? You think I'm afraid or ashamed of who I am?"

Jeannine straightened her back and looked at the black and white versions of herself. "Go away, both of you. You are parts of who I am, but you are not the whole."

The different versions of Jeannine looked confused, then turned questioningly to Cassandra.

"Eyes front, ladies," said Jeannine. "I'm the one talking to you both. Fuck off. Now."

The images faded.

Cassandra looked angry.

"Mama, for the last couple of days I've been experiencing visions—seeing things like I did after Katrina. I'm sick of it, I'm sick of the visions, and I'm sick of you and Papa Nightmare and whoever else is playing in my head."

"And what are you going to do about it, Dearheart? Your path is already set. You chose it yourself."

"Really, Mama? Perhaps you shouldn't have given me *knowledge* with power. I know you and Ti Malice need me to *choose* to be the next Cassandra. Well, I choose freedom. From you, and from the Loa. I am *not* the next Cassandra. I am Jeannine LaRue."

"You cannot do this!" shrieked Cassandra, her ice-blue eyes wide in shock. The image of her mother changed, morphed. Cassandra's white karabela dress shredded and became stained, while the form within shrank to a pale, skeletal caricature of her mother.

Jeannine towered over her mother's shriveled remains.

"I can do whatever I want. And that's your

nightmare, isn't it? Being the last in the line of Cassandras. Getting *so* close to fulfilling your purpose and stumbling at the finish line. Well, you are in for one hell'uva surprise, bitch. Because now it's *my turn* to show all of *you* nightmares."

Jeannine sucked in a breath as she found herself back in the front passenger seat of the police SUV. Curtis yanked at her seat belt.

"Curtis! Stop, it's okay. Stop. I'm back," she said.

Curtis sat back. "Cassandra?"

"No, it's *me. Me* me. We have to move because . . . "

Jeannine was suddenly smothered in a bear hug.

"*Oof*. Okay. We . . . " She found herself hugging Curtis just as hard. She felt his shoulders sag, as if the weight of *everything* just lifted.

"I'm sorry," they both said at the same time. They laughed.

That's when they heard a light tapping. Easy Street stood at Jeannine's window holding Ms. Maxine's case.

"Whoa, man!" said Easy, backing away from the window, hands in the air. "Already been shot in the face. Twice, in fact. I might be dead, but I don't wanna do that again, you dig?"

"Easy's with me, Curtis. Put the gun away."

"You sure?" asked Curtis.

"Maybe," she replied. She got out of the car and stepped to her right, leaving Curtis with a clear shot at least. "I'm not sure what bullets would do to a dead man," she said, keeping her eyes on Easy Street. "But since you seem to be solid enough, I'm thinking an ex-Army Ranger might be able to take your head off, which would make it difficult to play Ms. Maxine. Am I right?"

Easy Street scowled at her.

"Did you get what I asked you for?" she queried.

"Yes, Ms. Jeannine."

"Where is it?"

"Where you asked me to put it," he replied.

"Curtis," said Jeannine, not taking her eyes off the jazzman. "Don't shoot him yet."

"You sure?" he asked for a second time.

"Yep."

"Ms. Jeannine," said Easy. "*She* knows you're here. She knows what you aim to be doing, dig?"

"We should get the rest of the krewe here, except for the traitor," said Curtis. The hatred in his voice made Jeannine wonder how long Gallow would walk the earth once Curtis got a hold of the man. But that was a worry for later.

"No time," Jeannine said. "Lead the way, Easy. Let's not keep Mama waiting, shall we?"

⚜

Left to their own devices, the undead officers had ripped a path all the way to the old asylum's entranceway. The skeletons stood still, at the ready, on either side of the black gateway. Morbid sentries, awaiting orders. Things were moving so fast, Jeannine hadn't had time to process the murder of the two cops. When the images of the two guards whose bones she'd ripped from their bodies screamed their way into her brain, her steps faltered. Curtis made as if to steady her, but she waved him off with a strained, "I'm fine."

But she knew she wasn't fine. Knew she never would be.

BAYOU WHISPERS

She wondered how Curtis and his boys did it. Lived with themselves after all the death and destruction they'd wrought. She knew Curtis drank too much, and after her plane ride, she wasn't sure if she was headed down the same alcohol-sodden path she'd been on in college. Stanley had gotten her clean and sober. One of his grand gestures that, on the surface, indicated he deeply cared. It was only later that she'd found out the reason he'd gotten involved with her sobriety was to make sure "his success story" stayed a success.

Her regret at trusting Stanley and shunning Curtis back then turned into guilt over the men she'd killed. Her thoughts spiraled. She needed to pull it together or her plan would never work.

The two policemen she had killed—she knew they had been coming to kill her. She saw it in their minds after she took the deal from her mother and the power of Ti Malice flowed through her. But the ends didn't justify the means. Knowing they were going to kill her didn't make it feel all right. Perhaps as a soldier it was easier to reconcile—kill or be killed. But she was an officer of the court, not a soldier. Justice was her weapon.

Jeannine told the bone officers to keep standing watch. The creatures hissed acknowledgement, eye sockets tracking Easy as he stumbled while clutching Ms. Maxine, Curtis following warily behind.

"They're with me," she said to the undead.

The hanging vines, the moss, and the trees nearly covered the entranceway to the psychiatric center. In a few more years, the bayou will have completely reclaimed the man-made structure.

No one would ever know that a building had been here.

"This is her home, Ms. Jeannine," said Easy, his voice interrupting her thoughts and emotions. He stood looking at her. His sunglasses hid any expression.

Her mother's room was overgrown with invaders. Roots twisted among the chairs, and a bedside hospital table lay on its side, fully enveloped in moss. The drop ceiling, completely opened to the chases and ducts above it, had begun to disintegrate as the bayou asserted dominance. Insects darted to and fro in massive clouds, and an incessant buzz surrounded them all.

Jeannine wondered, as she looked at the dispassionate Easy Street, if the maggots in his eyes knew what the ghoulish jazzman was thinking.

"You said this is where your mother's physical form is," said Curtis. "I can't imagine any person living in here. Maybe a family of snapping turtles. But I haven't heard any birds or animals, come to think of it. Have you?"

"No," said Jeannine. She was doubting herself again. "Just insects. A lot more in here than anywhere else we've seen." *This feels . . . wrong.*

"Maybe we should regroup and think this through better," said Curtis. "You know, a full-blown plan with contingencies."

"No. Mama is weak," replied Jeannine. "When I rejected her power, it damaged her somehow. I don't know how to explain it better than that."

Curtis frowned, and Jeannine could see he was upset at having his idea dismissed, but he remained silent.

Easy was more thoughtful. "She is here, Ms. Jeannine, and it's true, she knows you are coming, but with this." Easy held up Ms. Maxine's case. "She can't see our thoughts."

"Easy's right," said Jeannine. "There may be no better time to end this—or at least end Cassandra before she wakes Ti Malice. We go now."

"Should we bring the Argonauts over there as backup?" asked Curtis, as he pointed toward the remains of the two cops standing watch.

"She controls the dead like Papa Nightmare does," shuddered Easy. "She's weak, but still has some power. She could turn those two on us."

"How do we fight them if that happens?" asked Jeannine.

"Take off their heads. Breaks the magic that binds them," replied the jazzman.

"So, that would work on you too, then?" said Jeannine as she felt along the edge of the cypress.

Easy swallowed and said nothing.

"I'll take that as a "yes." That's good info. So, you're right, we should act now." Her hand felt cold metal. "Ah!"

Jeannine raised an ancient machete in her hands. She turned it over slowly, feeling its weight. *She tried to kill me with this.*

And now Jeannine planned on returning the favor.

Jeannine broke out in a cold sweat. This had been her *mother*. A monster, sure. An evil bitch, no doubt. But at one point, in the distant past, this twisted creature had raised and nurtured her.

It was only now, near the end, that Jeannine realized this "Cassandra" was finally in complete control. That her mother was truly gone.

Little Jeannine came into the house, crying. The other children had been so mean. Her mother made lemonade and they sat on the stoop as Jeannine's tormentors—white boys and girls—played tag. Cassandra called to them and, to young Jeannine's embarrassment, asked them to include her in the game.

The biggest boy—Jeannine couldn't remember his name—called her a whore and a nigger while the others laughed.

Cassandra told her little girl not to worry. That sticks and stones . . . et cetera.

But the words stung. Made Jeannine feel ashamed.

Cassandra told her stories of good black and white folks. She told her some people were stupid and ignorant. That what's-his-name was a racist.

Jeannine cried herself to sleep that night.

When Jeannine woke the next morning, the neighborhood was abuzz. A white boy had been attacked by a pack of dogs early in the morning. The animals had torn him limb from limb.

Jeannine was glad.

Her mother never said a word about it, but from that point forward, her mother became distant.

Different.

How had her mother justified killing that child? The now-adult Jeannine knew that's exactly what Cassandra had done. Her mother had called upon the magic of Ti Malice, who was always willing to accept more blood.

Now she, Jeannine, was going to kill what was left of her mother.

Another *murder*, for that's what it was. She could pretend to justify the death of the cops—they were going to kill her; she wasn't in full control of her own mind—whatever. But this was murder. Cassandra had tried to kill her—a couple of times. But Jeannine was in full control of her body and mind now.

This was murder.

And she'd have to live with that.

"Where did you find it?" asked Jeannine, holding up the machete.

"Ask me no questions and I won't lie to ya, dig?" replied Easy. He flashed that bright white grin of his.

"Well, thank you, Easy," she said. "Be careful. If Mama knows we're here, she's probably laid traps everywhere. She may not be able to read our thoughts, but she's smart and ruthless."

She looked at the machete in her hands, feeling the weight of the blade.

I'll figure out a way to live with this, too.

"Let's go cut the evil bitch's head off," she said, and set off for the ruins of the insane asylum.

The grin never left Easy's face.

TWENTY-ONE

U-Store-It!
Public Self-Storage Units off of Interstate 12

WHILE FERNÁNDEZ SPENT the night alternating between stacking crap in front of the big metal door and bitching under his breath about "lazy-ass magic douchebags," Roo prepared for the reanimation of Charley Mouton. The spell used to create the clay vessel for the Golem was relatively straight forward and was to be the last component of the invocation to be done closest to dawn. Using Charley's degraded tooth to return the ex-Ranger's soul to the created body, that was the tricky part.

Besides, Roo thought, as Fernández swore loudly because the cot he'd just tossed on the top of the makeshift barrier tumbled off the pile and nearly hit him, hard work helps the little man forget he's been out of chewing tobacco for a few hours.

A little before dawn, the bit of yellowing ivory that represented what was left of Charley's physical form, hummed with stored energy as Roo completed the difficult spell work. Next, Roo prepared the clay version of Charley and set up the candles and items that had been important to the Golem in his former life: a picture of him fishing with his father when he was six years old, his Coke-bottle glasses, his regiment ring, and his purple heart. These items were required to transfer the Golem's soul into his new clay form.

Fernández commented that the new body looked a bit bigger than the last one.

"You have no idea," said Roo to the smaller man's observation.

All that was needed were the Hebrew prayer and words that would finish the summoning.

Fernández never knew Roo had obtained so much knowledge of religion. Sure, he knew of Roo's obsession with the occult and with Voudon, but during the evening, he'd discussed the Kabbalah, Catholicism, Buddhism, and the schism between the Sunni and the Shiite Muslims. His friend was the "Google of Religion," as far as he could tell.

"We're ready then?" asked Fernández.

"Eh?"

He repeated himself a bit louder for Roo's sake.

"Yep," answered Roo. He pulled his smartphone from his pocket, checked on the timing of dawn, then kicked off the countdown timer app on his phone and watched the seconds tick away.

Less than thirty minutes before daybreak.

29:48 before daybreak

Fernández pulled his flip phone from his pocket. He tried to reach Curtis once again, but the number rang out and the boss's voicemail was now full. He tried Gallow next. The restaurateur picked up on the first ring.

"Where the hell have you been?" demanded Fernández, then listened to Gallow's reply for a moment. "Whoa! Hang on," he said. "Roo," called Fernández, "I got Gallow, finally. He says we've got a problem."

"No shit, we do," muttered Roo, as he set his phone on the hood of his truck so he could see the numbers from most anywhere in the storage unit. "He on speaker? Bring him here."

Fernández jogged over to the truck with his cell. As soon as he set it down, Roo picked it up and increased the volume. The speaker squawked once in protest.

"What's the problem, Carl?" asked Roo.

"The Major . . . he has Curtis and Jeannine. I don't know where. I was hauled off for questioning at the Orleans Parish . . . "

"That sounds like a problem, all right," replied Roo.

"It gets worse," said Gallow.

"Of course it does. Explain."

"They know where you guys are. The Major was screaming because he wanted the state police to scramble a SWAT team. From what I heard, the staties are refusing to get involved without the Parish Sheriff's Office say-so."

"That sounds like we've got some time, then," said Fernández.

"I don't think so. He made a few other calls, then left with a whole bunch of his jackbooted recruits. I really think you guys should get gone—like, now."

"Can't," said Roo. "Sunup is in less than a half hour. If I don't do the ritual, the Golem will be gone for real this time."

"Fuck Charley," spat Gallow. "He'd understand. Get out of there and save your asses. Otherwise the Major'll rough you guys up, sure. But eventually, he'll leave both of you alone. He gave his word. He only wants Jonesy and the girl."

Roo and Fernández looked at each other.

"The Major gave his word, did he? And how do you *know* the Major'll leave us alone, Carl?" asked Roo quietly.

The phone was silent for a moment.

"It's still dark out," said Roo. "Those undead things—all the ghoulies and ghosties and zonbis—all work a lot better in the dark, don't they, Gallow?"

Even with his ears as bad as they are, Roo heard Gallow swallow, making the speaker crackle again.

"Yeah, don't answer that. I've been studying this shit for decades, man," said Roo. "These . . . things . . . are creatures of the night, of the dark. They don't like the sun very much."

"Done a deal with the Major *and* that lunatic Papa Nightmare, haven't you, *puta de mierda?*" snarled Fernández.

"Look," said Gallow quickly. "Bad shit is heading your way, right now. Cut a deal. After Jonesy fucked us with the armored car heist, I cut a deal. I'm still sucking in oxygen and will be for years. I have a restaurant to think about. Think about your future. The writing is on the wall, guys. Between Papa

Nightmare and the Major, the little guys are being squeezed out of the racket. You know what a ruthless bastard the Major is! We'd be sitting at the bottom of the bayou stuffed in a 55-gallon drum if we kept going the—"

"Traitor," said Fernández.

"Always knew you was a slimy cocksucker, Gallow. Just never thought you'd sell out your own brothers. Guess I was wrong about that."

"You set us up," said Fernández through gritted teeth. "Back at Roo's place. It was a fucking setup. *Voy a cortar tu corazon!*" he shouted into the cell.

Roo held up his hand.

"Listen to me good, you two-faced prick. I'm gonna let Lil' Dave cut out your heart, I promise you. Especially if Jonesy and Jeannine are hurt. But we're gonna make you suffer first. That's what we do to traitors. Remember Bogotá?"

"Traitor!" screamed Fernández.

"Don't say I didn't warn you both," replied Gallow. "Good luck with what's heading your way."

Fernández threw his cell across the storage unit. It shattered against the wall.

He realized he was breathing heavily and focused on shoving his anger aside. He focused on the clay body of the Golem.

"What do we do now, Roo?" he asked, not taking his eyes off Charley. He knew, if he looked at Roo, he'd see the same pain he was feeling.

"Now, we prepare to be invaded," whispered Roo. "I ain't leaving the Golem."

Roo always knew what was right. Fernández nodded.

"Fuckin' A, man. Let's get to work."

BAYOU WHISPERS

21:22 before daybreak

They'd just finished handloading Roo's last two assault rifles, setting them within easy reach, when a banging erupted on the storage unit's big metal garage door.

"Do you think it's Jehovah's Witnesses?" asked Fernández as he lifted an M16 on his shoulder.

"Cops would've used the bullhorn first, or rang my cell," said Roo, adjusting his own weapon. "They wouldn't have knocked."

The banging got louder, as if one fist had turned to many.

"That's not right," said Fernández, frowning, raising the weapon Roo had given him. "Shouldn't they be trying to negotiate our surrender or something?"

Roo's phone rang as if on cue. The timer to sunrise moved to the upper left and read 20:41. *Only twenty goddamn minutes. Stall them.*

Roo answered the phone.

"Hello, this is Richard "Red Rooster" Romain speaking. To whom do I have the pleasure of speaking—"

"I will make this pledge to you," said a smooth, deep voice. "Your and your companion's death will be swift if you come out now. Otherwise? Well, my men can be rather brutal."

"Who the hell is this?"

"Some call me Papa Nightmare. That is certainly what I am to you this morning. But I can also be merciful. Come out and I will make your deaths quick and painless."

Roo had never heard the man speak before. He'd only heard the stories, stories of terror and torture for pleasure. Stories of death—and worse than death.

His throat went dry, as a chill raced up and down his spine.

Papa fucking Nightmare is here.

The pounding on the metal increased, becoming chaotic, frantic. Muffled, unintelligible voices mixed with animalistic hisses and snarls. The same sounds he'd heard from those zonbis ripping apart Bernstein's SUV.

Something—or more accurately—some *things* wanted in.

"Why don't you go out to the highway and play "hide and go fuck yourself"?" he replied and hit "end."

"That was quick," muttered Fernández.

"We have a date later. He was tellin' me about his dress. It was Papa Nightmare. Remember how you were all worried about maybe having to shoot some cops?"

The garage door buckled. Metal screamed in protest and the hinged panels began to separate.

Pre-dawn light shown through the gaps.

"Yeah," said Fernández worriedly. "Cops."

"I don't think that's gonna be an issue for you," said Roo, as he glanced again at his alarm. They had to hold the storage facility for about twenty more minutes. He calmly flicked the select-fire switch on his weapon to "full automatic."

The door gave way with a loud screech. Metal and the stacked contents of the storage facility flew in all directions. Blue and grey undead swarmed into the space. Zombie infantry men opened up with Springfields and Whitworths. A couple of enterprising young ghouls busied themselves setting up a Gatling gun.

Game on, thought Roo again as he and Fernández opened up on the invaders at the exact same time.

12:33 before daybreak

They were almost out of ammo.

The undead were former soldiers, but they were now under the command of Papa Nightmare—someone who, Roo now knew, while brutal and merciless, was inexperienced as a military leader. The Voudon priest was used to a brute-force approach. The number of dismantled Civil War-era corpses piled up in the storage unit was a testament to Papa Nightmare's lack of military acumen.

Roo and Fernández had pushed the zombies out of the storage unit once. After dismembering the initial attackers, they'd used Roo's truck as a tank, ramming anything wearing blue or grey. The vehicle had given its life for the two men and the soon-to-be-awakened Golem. Riddled with a couple dozen bullet holes, steam rose from the deceased engine. Two tires had been summarily shredded by nineteenth-century weapons fire, and the zombies were lining up for a final push.

Papa Nightmare might have been inexperienced, but he learned fast.

Roo, Fernández, and what would hopefully become the Golem were in the bed of the pickup. It was a miracle that neither Roo nor Fernández had been seriously wounded. Fernández had a gash across one cheek from a sabre, while Roo had nothing more than a wrenched knee.

"Not bad," panted Fernández, "for a couple of old vets."

"I need to get the ritual going," hissed Roo amid more bullets slamming into the sheet metal. "The truck's armor plating should hold off most of the lead flying our way. It's now or never."

Fernández vehemently nodded his head and fired his last couple of rounds. He put the rifle down and picked up an axe. The meaning was clear: *I've got your back, whatever it takes.*

Fernández is a good man, thought Roo.

Roo crouched over Charley and began the *leyn,* reciting a verse from the Torah in Hebrew, then—in that singsong voice that emphasized the high and low tones dating back to the time of Ezra—he began the last chorus. Eleven phrases. That's all. Eleven.

"*Aleph-Alef! Aleph-Bet! Aleph-Gimel! Aleph-Dalet!Aleph-H . . . !*"

07:03 before daybreak

A zombie soldier in Union blue rushed at the truck, climbing a small mound of corpses of its fallen comrades.

Fernández took its head off with a well-timed swing of the axe.

What is Papa Nightmare doing? Thought Roo. *Why isn't he taking the time to reorganize his line?*

Of course! The lighter it gets, the less control he has over the undead in the real world!

If Roo could finish the ritual, they'd have enough help to send this entire undead party back to wherever Nightmare hid the ghost ship *Sultana*. Roo continued to give his summoning extra power. He hoped the Golem would like his new strength, since this fight would need so much more than the one where he died.

Six more phrases.

"Aleph-Vav! Aleph-Zayin! Aleph-Chet! Aleph-Tet! Aleph-Yod . . . !"

02:38 before daybreak

A final desperate push of Papa Nightmare's zonbi army began as the sky quickly changed from black to purple to gold tinged.

Soldiers poured into the storage unit. Many holding sabers and clubs. A few old rifles opened up on the two former Rangers.

Covered in sweat and zonbi, Fernández dove for cover, stealing a glance at Roo. His heart leapt to his throat.

Roo lay next to the Golem, blood streaming from multiple wounds. His coloring had turned ashen and his eyes were glassy. Roo's mouth was moving, but Fernández couldn't hear any sounds from his friend.

The bed of the pickup smelled of death.

Ghouls scrambled toward Fernández. He redoubled his grip on the ax.

I'm ready.

Through the noise and the chaos, Fernández heard his buddy's last gasp:

Aleph-Kaf!

Blood seeped from Roo's mouth, nose, and ears. His head turned to one side.

Fernández watched him die.

Screaming with white-hot fury, Fernández stood, raised his axe high above his head. He swung at the undead with wild abandon, cutting down any creature trying to get at Roo's body.

The sun broke the horizon, bathing the storage unit in golden, smoke-defused light.

00:07 before daybreak

Fernández screamed again as a dozen of the creatures overwhelmed his position.

From the back of the pickup truck came an unearthly roar that answered Fernández's scream. Zonbis flew out of the bed in all directions. The roar sounded again, so loud it shook the storage unit and stopped the undead in their tracks.

The Golem was awake.

00:00 daybreak

TWENTY-TWO

Bayou Cypress Pavilion for the Criminally Insane
New Orleans

T HEY WAITED UNTIL daybreak to explore the ruined psychiatric center.

Curtis tried Roo and Fernández one last time, leaving a message.

"Roo, if you get this, J and I are free and we're at Cass's place. Come when you can. Gallow's in bed with the Major. Watch your asses."

Curtis put the cell back in his pocket. Two calls—to Roo and Fernández, leaving two identical voicemails. Dawn had broken and he hoped his two *compadres* were okay—and that they'd been able to quietly bring back the Golem.

I'm not sure what will piss Charley off more—the amount of shit he's missed in the last twenty-four hours, or the fact that Gallow betrayed us. How did I not see that coming? Georgina always hated him, refused to eat at his restaurant even.

Jeannine spent an hour adjusting her prosthetic. "It's the humidity. Makes the stump swell."

It was the only thing she'd said to Jones all morning.

When she was done, she stomped off toward the

181

ruined building, Easy Street following in her wake. The ghoul had cast one look Curtis's way before following her. At least, Curtis thought it was his way. It was hard to tell where an eyeless dead jazzman was looking.

Curtis had hung back to make his calls, allowing the other two to examine the rotting, fetid entranceway that sat at the end of what used to be a courtyard. The bayou had reclaimed that space and was well on its way to devouring the entire complex. Watching the two of them poke around the entrance, the weight of the last day's events made him suddenly feel weak-kneed. He leaned on the stolen police SUV for support. It wasn't from any physical pain that caused his weariness—in fact, he felt fantastic. But any physical pain would be more welcome compared to the emotional and mental anguish tearing at his soul.

She sounds like Jeannine, but is she?

Sure, he was aware there was some strange shit in the world. Acceptance of that fact didn't necessarily beget full-on belief in the supernatural, though. That was Roo's department. Maybe Fernández's and the traitor's, as well. He'd *accepted* the fact of Charley's remaking—the Golem was walking around, wasn't he? He'd *accepted* the spirit of Cassandra—he'd spoken with her, and she'd led him to Jeannine after the girl had escaped from those bayou rats, hadn't she?

But this transformation of Jeannine. She'd said she was Cassandra, then she'd said she wasn't. She didn't know a damn thing about this voodoo stuff before, and now she spoke with the dead and planned on more killing.

BAYOU WHISPERS

She killed two cops.

She told me to call her Cassandra.

Then she told me she was sorry—exactly what I wanted to hear. Maybe she really is Jeannine. But I can't help but feel I'm being played.

Being betrayed by one of his own tended to ratchet his paranoia to an "eleven."

Fucking Carl Gallow, that bastard.

The entire asylum smelled of terror and death. He knew what happened in this facility during and right after Katrina. A lot of places—jails, asylums, and slums, mostly—were abandoned by those charged with keeping people in such places safe. He saw first-hand how people were treated by those with power again and again during his different tours of duty.

Death was ready to welcome him through the crumbling maw that had once been a doorway. He'd been ready for death since the war. More so since Georgina's passing. He was tired of living, of the constant state of alert. He wanted to rest. Oh, God, how he wanted to rest. But he had to see it through . . . whatever this shit with Jeannine, Cassandra, and the Loa was.

A dark thought seeped into his brain, making his blood feel like ice in his veins. What if his death came at the hands of someone he always thought of as a daughter?

Get a hold of yourself, Jones.

Regardless, death was coming. A feeling of dread had hung over him for months. It used to just hover in the background. A constant hum, like a mosquito buzzing around his head. But ever since the accident—seeing Randy, seeing those zombies, seeing Bernstein—the feeling of his imminent doom was in the forefront of his brain.

A shout snapped him from his brooding thoughts.

"Curtis!" called Jeannine. She'd stopped before crossing the ruined threshold.

Time to play this out.

Curtis joined Jeannine and Easy in surveying the entrance to the ruins.

To him, the building felt like a cross between a swamp and a graveyard. The combination made his skin crawl. He didn't know why, as he'd been in both many times. Except, this time, he knew for certain there was something evil across the threshold.

The trio entered the building and a veil of silence enveloped them. The only things that moved or made a sound were the clouds of insects that descended upon them, happy to have a new food supply to nibble. The mosquitos were the worst. Hovering around his face like a beekeeper's mask. The last time he'd been surrounded by so many bugs was when he'd found Jeannine after Katrina.

Best not to think of that now.

The bugs avoided Easy, Curtis noticed.

Smart critters.

There was an energy here. A malevolence that oozed like dampness and permeated every part of this place. The bayou was reclaiming the building and grounds, for sure. But something else was reclaiming the damned soul of this place.

"I don't like this place," he said, realizing after that he'd said it aloud.

"It's Cassandra, and Ti Malice," answered Jeannine. "They own this place. They're changing it into something they feel comfortable in." She glanced at Curtis, her ice-blue eyes full of concern. "This is what they have planned for the whole planet."

BAYOU WHISPERS

Chaotic streams of light filtered in as the dawn took hold. Various holes in the roof and walls cast insane shadows around them. Motes of dust and swarms of insects danced in the light. Curtis wondered if the tiny creatures knew something malevolent lurked deeper in the shattered asylum.

Jeannine cocked her head to one side—a motion Curtis saw out of the corner of his eye. "What's wrong?" he asked.

"Singing. Can you hear it?"

"It's Blue Sue," said Easy. "Someone I knew when I was alive," he added in response to the look on Curtis's face.

"No," said Jeannine. "It's my mother. It's that old hymn she used to sing. It's coming from that hallway over there," she said, as she pointed at a gaping door frame infested with vines.

"I don't hear anything," said Curtis. "She took over your mind once. She'll try again. Are you ready?"

"The mother-Cassandra is too weak. She hasn't even tried to manifest," replied Jeannine. "It's just the singing, calling to us. Can't you hear it?"

"All I hear is the buzzing of bugs and water dripping from somewhere," said Curtis.

"This way." Jeannine lifted the machete and walked away as if she hadn't heard him.

Easy followed her at a distance, stopping at a stagnant pool of water by the remains of the front desk.

"Let's go, dead man," called Curtis.

Easy looked at him and smiled.

"What's so funny?" asked Curtis.

"Private joke, dig?"

I'm angry, confused, and frightened, and this

185

som'bitch is laughing about it. Fear was a good thing. It meant his senses were heightened, his ability to react increased. He might be sixty, but decades of military and civilian police training would kick in, he was sure of it. He should be exhausted. But he felt more alive than he had in years. *Must be the adrenaline of a mission.*

He watched Jeannine examine the opening to a hallway, the details of which were hidden in shadow. *I hope I can protect her when the time comes.*

I hope she can resist Cassandra.

Bones lay scattered across what was once a large reception area. Not human bones, though. Animals. Dogs, boars, and alligators. Large birds—herons or egrets, most likely.

Curtis bent low to examine a particularly large skull.

"These bones," he said. "They all have marks on them. Teeth marks, but it doesn't make sense."

He shifted the large skull to better see the marks. Large insects scurried in all directions, upset their home had been disturbed.

"I think these are snake bite marks," he said. "But the spacing isn't right. It's massive. We don't have anything this big, even down here. I mean I've heard of boas being found in the Everglades—rich people flushing their pets when they get bored of them, sort of thing . . . "

"I saw a snake this big once," interrupted Jeannine, a faraway look in her eyes. "I was on the roof of my Nana's home during Katrina. I was all alone. The water had taken her and . . . " Jeannine's voice broke. "I saw a friend of mine, tried to grab her when this big black snake snatched her away from me."

Jeannine suddenly turned her back on Curtis and Easy.

"That snake," she whispered. "The fucking thing smiled at me when it stole my friend."

Curtis put his hand on her shoulder. "You were a kid. Frightened. You don't know . . . "

She spun on him. "I know what I saw!"

"Okay, okay," he said, removing his arm before she decided to separate it from his body with the machete. "So, like, what? An anaconda? They're in South America."

"No idea," she said angrily. "All I know is I saw it. It smiled. It ate my friend."

For a moment Curtis's expression softened. Then he tossed the skull on the ground and said, "Let's get this thing with your mother over with."

"I couldn't agree more. I think . . . she's that way." Jeannine pointed to an opening that must have once held a large pair of wooden doors. Only the rusted bits of the hardware remained strewn about the other detritus on the floor.

"How do you know?" asked Curtis.

"I . . . just do," she said.

"I guess that way it is," he replied, and walked in the direction she pointed.

Jeannine followed.

"C'mon, jazzman," said Curtis, noticing the ghoul had fallen behind to examine the skull. Easy hurried to catch up without a word.

They found themselves in an old corridor. The ceiling tiles had long ago collapsed and turned into little more than putrid slag from years of being open to the elements. There was less light than in the lobby—just one shattered skylight above what was once a nurse's station, and diffused lighting from nearby patient rooms where glass had been knocked out and cypress trees had grown in through the window frames and between cinder blocks. Behind the built-in desk of the former nurse's station sat an office chair covered in mold and weeds. On the desk itself, the only thing recognizable was a telephone encased in moss. Wherever Curtis looked, the modern things of mankind were slowly being consumed by an unforgiving bayou.

"The music is getting louder," said Jeannine.

Curtis would have to take her word for it.

Jeannine and Curtis searched each room along the hall, one at a time. Most were ruined shells—plaster sloughed to the floor; bloated fiberboard ceiling tiles in wet piles where they'd fallen; and overturned equipment carts covered in vines, roots, and weeds.

Easy stood in the hall watching them go in and out of the rooms, not bothering to search. "There ain't nothing worth anything here, dig?" he'd said when Curtis commented on his lack of help.

In the second-to-last room before the stairwell, a pile of what looked like rags lay on the floor. Curtis had already dismissed the pile as just another decaying bit of garbage and had turned to leave when Jeannine said, "Wait."

At the sound of her voice, the pile stirred.

"Jesus Christ!" said Curtis. He put his arm in front of Jeannine, as if to block her from the rags.

She placed a hand on his arm and slowly lowered it.

The pile of rags shook, then rose.

It was a skeleton wearing a filthy, moth-eaten hospital gown. White, moss-encrusted wisps of hair hung from a head little more than a skull.

Folds of leather opened where the eye sockets were.

Ice-blue eyes stared from the skull.

"Hello, daughter," rasped the remains.

TWENTY-THREE

U-Store-It!
Public Self-Storage Units off of Interstate 12

CHARLEY "THE GOLEM" MOUTON had taken out a dozen zombie soldiers before the undead creatures knew they were in trouble. He'd picked up Roo's truck and used it as a massive sledgehammer to pound them into dust.

"Golem," yelled Fernández, as a couple of the undead turned from the resurrected Charley to renew their attack on him.

The Golem moved toward Fernández and tore the heads off the would-be attackers.

Fernández picked up the axe that had fallen from his hands during the onslaught, and he and the Golem prepared to charge at the remaining zonbi soldiers.

The sharp blast of a horn startled them.

The undead turned and retreated from the storage unit.

Fernández and the Golem chased after the blue and grey ghouls. The Golem ran in a sideways lope reminiscent of a large primate and roared at the top of his lungs. Fernández moved as quickly as he could to catch up and was so focused on the pumping of his legs that he nearly slammed into the Golem when the bigger man stopped dead in his tracks.

"Holy Mary, Mother of God," said the Golem.

Fernández poked his head out from behind Charley.

On the unnamed waterway of the Mississippi that ran behind the U-Store-It! complex sat a dilapidated, burnt husk of a paddle wheeler. Through the soot, they could make out one word on the side of the ship.

Sultana.

The Civil War ghouls boarded the vessel via a series of wooden planks, and a large man, naked from the waist up, waved a mock greeting at the ex-Rangers.

Papa Nightmare.

The boat vanished in the blink of an eye.

"*Dios mio.* That was that boat Roo told us about. The one that exploded," said Fernández. He began to shake as the adrenaline coursing through his veins now had no one left to fight.

"I'm gonna smash that fucker to paste one day," growled the Golem. "C'mon, Dave, let's get back inside. We gotta collect what we can and get out of here."

"Fuck," screamed Fernández at the top of his lungs, as he threw the axe toward where the *Sultana* once sat. "Fuck. Gallow told us the Major was on his way here. Then that Voodoo asshole shows up instead. Nightmare is definitely in cahoots with the Major," said Fernández.

"Us?" asked the Golem.

"Shit—Roo!" said Fernández, and ran back toward the storage unit, the Golem on his heels.

"Oh, no. Oh, my God," said the Golem when he saw Roo's body.

Fernández fell to his knees. He placed a hand on Roo's bloody forehead.

"He saved us both, Charley. Rangers lead the way, don't they?" he said.

"Jesus . . . " replied the Golem.

They heard a buzzing and Roo's cellphone, its cracked screen face-up and speckled with blood, lit up: *1 New Voicemail from Jonesy*

"We'll have to mourn later. There's shit going down," said Fernández, picking up the phone.

The Golem nodded. "Survival comes first. We'll get them for this. I promise."

"Damn straight, we will," replied Fernández as he tried to open the phone's voicemail.

Face Not Recognized

"Fuck, he's got some sort of face recognition thing."

"Actually, it's the eyes," said the Golem.

"What?"

"The phone says facial whatever. But it's really just the eyes. Roo told me once."

Fernández looked over at his late friend, face covered in blood.

Eyes wide open in death.

"Damn it," said Fernández, swallowing down a sob that threatened to break free and overwhelm him. He knelt next to Roo's corpse. He wiped away most of the blood and held the phone in front of his friend's lifeless face.

The screen unlocked.

Fernández touched the "voicemail" icon but nothing happened.

"Damn it," he said again, and wiped the blood from the screen, then his hands on his shirt.

Fernández selected the voicemail icon again, and Curtis's voice filled the storage unit.

"Roo, if you get this, J and I are free and we're at Cass's place. Come when you can. Gallow's in bed with the Major, watch your asses."

"What the fuck does that mean?" asked the Golem.

"It means Jonesy and Jeannine are in trouble at that fucking insane asylum," said Fernández as he stood. He placed Roo's cell in his pocket.

"And Gallow in bed with that fucktard Major?" asked the Golem.

"Yeah, that's pretty fucking self-explanatory," replied Fernández. For the first time in his life, he understood what the phrase "seeing red" meant. Anger and pain were on the verge of overwhelming him.

The Golem punched the wreckage of Roo's truck, sliding it ten feet across the floor.

I guess I have to be the voice of reason for once, thought Fernández. He took a breath. *Think. What would Jonesy do?*

He'd get the hell out of Dodge, is what Jonesy'd do.

"Okay. First, we have to find a ride. You did a number on Roo's truck."

"What about Roo's body?" the Golem asked.

"Let's see if we can find his cousin. Maybe he'll help with this mess."

"There are Civil War zombie parts all over the place along with Roo's dead body in here, Fernández. Pretty sure his cousin is not gonna want anything to do with this."

"We'll have to be persuasive, then."

Fernández walked back over to Roo's body and knelt. "I'm gonna use your phone for a bit, man. I hope you don't mind. We'll come back for you, I promise."

He closed his friend's eyes.

"Okay. First things first," said Fernández, looking up at the Golem. "Do you remember what Roo's cousin's name is?"

❖

"I'm gonna kill both of you assholes."

Fernández and the Golem found Roo's cousin, Tyrone, in the storage facility's office. Charley had suggested the cousin's name "might be Timmy, but I really wasn't listening." Getting the man's name wrong was the least of their problems now.

Roo's cousin looked like a bald version of their late friend. From the exact same dark skin tone to the wild, bug-eyed look when angry. He even pointed a mean-looking shotgun at Fernández's face the way Roo used to.

"Whoa, man!" said Fernández, both hands up. "Let's talk this out, okay?"

"You *killed my cousin*," said Tyrone. "There is nothing more to—"

"The zombies killed your cousin," said the Golem. His arms were folded across his chest and he sounded bored. "And we killed them back, so please, Timmy . . . "

"Tyrone!"

"Whatever. Put the gun down. All the noise we just made in the back of your lot is gonna bring down every cop in a hundred-mile radius on this place. And the only person they'll find here, not counting the zombie corpses and your cousin Roo, is you. Which means they'll come down on you like a ton of bricks. Cops. Against you—one angry black guy with a shotgun. Now, I'm not a betting man, but if I were, I'd bet on them not buying your story about two guys smashing Civil War zombies with your cousin's Ford pickup."

"*You* did that," muttered Fernández. "I was *shooting* the undead guys."

Sirens sounded in the distance. A distant *whump-whump* of helicopter blades grew closer, too.

"Dead bodies everywhere, including your cousin," said the Golem to Tyrone. "Do the math, man. Is there any equation that works in your favor?"

Tyrone lowered the shotgun a bit. "No."

"So, burn the office and get out of here," said Fernández, fidgeting in exasperation. "Or stay. I don't really care, but you can hear the sirens and the helicopter, right? It's decision time, *hombre*."

"And what're you assholes gonna do?" asked Tyrone.

"After you give us your keys, we're gonna take your car and lead the cops away from you. Should give you enough time to get to Mississippi."

"Why the fuck do I wanna be in Mississippi?"

I should just kill him and go, thought Fernández. Instead, he said, "Get to Biloxi. There is a guy by the name of Cain who works at the Margaritaville Resort. Tell him you're Roo's cousin and that Lil' Dave Fernández said you need to be gone yesterday. He'll take care of you."

The sirens grew louder. The chopper was nearly overhead.

"What about my family?" asked Tyrone, the sweat appearing on his forehead having nothing to do with the rising morning heat.

"Get them fast. Cain will move them, too."

"Think your friend Curtis would mind if I borrowed his Mercedes? Seein' as you're takin' my old Chevy," said Tyrone tossing Fernández the keys.

"Curtis? Mercedes?" asked Fernández.

"He came by here yesterday. Said he pinched it. It's in his storage unit."

"Fuckin' Curtis," said Fernández, shaking his head. "Yeah. Take it. It's hot, though."

"I already put Texas tags on it."

The chopper passed over the storage facility, slowing its forward momentum.

"We have to move. The chopper is here," said the Golem.

Fernández and Charley made their way toward the Chevy Impala parked next to the office when Charley turned back to Roo's cousin.

"Timmy!"

"Tyrone!"

"Yeah, whatever. Will the office fire take care of any video camera archive footage?"

"Shit, man. The cameras were there for show. Never hooked them up."

TWENTY-FOUR

Bayou Cypress Pavilion for the Criminally Insane
New Orleans

"MAMA?" CROAKED JEANNINE. The sound of her voice echoed dully in the ruins of the asylum.

The corpse-thing that had been Cassandra LaRue began a side-shuffling, slow limp toward them. Beetles and roaches streamed from underneath rotted clothing.

"That's far enough," said Curtis, when the creature had closed the distance between them to five feet. He produced a pistol he'd taken from the body of one of the Major's guards.

Jeannine saw the gun and knew there was only one place Curtis could have gotten it. *Cops. They were cops. She killed two cops. Dirty or no, they were— stop it! Not now.*

The creature let out a moist sound that could have been a laugh. The remaining skin on the left side of its jaw sloughed off and the mandible dislocated.

Cassandra-corpse didn't notice.

"The Major's men are Nazis, for lack of a better label," she rasped. "You shouldn't feel guilty about killing Nazis, Dear-heart." The skull with the ice-blue eyes turned to Curtis. "And you can't finish me with a gun, soldier—"

Curtis emptied the twelve-round magazine into what was left of Cassandra's chest.

Jeannine screamed as bits of old fabric, dust, leathered skin, and bone flew in all directions.

The echoes of gunfire faded. Smoke hung unmoving in the moist air like a death shroud on a corpse, and the acrid scent of gunpowder filled the air.

Cassandra gave out another wet laugh. The creature continued its bizarre, shuffling gait toward them, albeit at a slower pace. As the corpse shuffled across the floor, bits of it—including its jaw and half of its skull—dropped to the ground.

"Only complete removal of my head can finish me, boy. Didn't quite get all of it, did you?" The creature shook its head and more skull fragments dropped to the old asylum floor.

"What do you want, Mother?" asked Jeannine. She was terrified, but she couldn't let the remains of her mother know that. As she tried to close off her mind, her own ice-blue eyes locked on to the matching pair in the shattered remains of her mother's skull.

They were mirrors of one another. One set belonging to a disheveled attorney, the other to the monster that had been her mother.

Despite missing half its head, Cassandra's eyes shone bright from some internal light.

Jeannine felt her mother trying to get into her head. Slimy tendrils of thought emanated from her mother, caressing Jeannine's memories, trying to find a way past them to her inner thoughts.

"Show it the sword-thing," said Curtis to Jeannine.

Jeannine held up the machete and the creature stopped moving. It cocked its head to one side and appeared to consider the weapon.

"How perfect! I tried to kill you with that weapon," said Cassandra. "Now you've brought it here to cut off my head, haven't you? Retribution."

"What do you want?" repeated Jeannine.

"I want what I told you I wanted during my visit to your cement cage—to give you my power. Only then can my bones finally rest."

"I don't understand. I thought you were . . . still alive."

"You rejected me, Dear-heart," hissed the dead thing with the ice-blue eyes. "I'd poured most of what I, Cassandra, am—or was—into you. It was my final gift! My blessing for you to take my place as the final Cassandra. There has always been a Cassandra serving Ti Malice since her long sleep began. She nears wakefulness, so it is time for you to perform the Cassandras' last service to their master. That was never my role to undertake. I understand that now."

"How could you do any of the Loa's bidding if you're dead?"

"Ti Malice . . . needed to teach me a lesson. I wanted the glory of the final sacrifice. You didn't deserve the honor, I did! But that wasn't what Ti Malice wanted. She needed to punish me, Dear-heart."

"Punish you? Why?"

"For my failures, of course," hissed Cassandra. "And my arrogance."

The creature tried to shuffle toward them again when what was left of its left leg collapsed into dust. The creature grabbed onto a nearby rusted old headboard. The sound of metal hitting metal caused Jeannine to notice a pair of rusted handcuffs attached to what was left of the hospital bed. The mattress was long gone, but the rest of the plastic and metal bed frame still held what little weight Cassandra's ruined body possessed.

Jeannine had the impression the creature's skull was smiling at her.

"Ah! I see you noticed my former restraints. Yes, they worked quite well." She held up what was left of her hand, turning it over as if examining it. "Worked well. For a while, that is.

"They left me, you see. They were scared of me. Scared of the storm I'd brought to their doorstep."

"The storm *you* brought?"

"Yes, Dear-heart. The hurricane. Ti Malice gave me the power to turn the storm from the Gulf where it was supposed to die. Instead, I convinced the storm to come back to me. The bayou whispered to me, told me how to breathe life into the clouds and the rain. So much death. So much blood. Ti Malice was close to waking that day. We were so close. Let me show you."

The wind howled. Staff scrambled, trying to save important records, while the rest of the papers fell to the floor. Small equipment that could be carried was taken, the larger pieces left, shoved into corners and rooms that were empty because the patients had been moved.

But not all the patients would be leaving.

Cassandra, still handcuffed to her bed, watched as others being taken to safety were escorted down the hall, their asses hanging out of their gowns.

BAYOU WHISPERS

A shadow fell across her vision. The silhouette of a menacing figure blocked most of the doorway. For a second, she thought she was going to safety, too. But the big brute of a man approached her with a second pair of handcuffs, attaching her ankle to the bed. When she began to scream, he shoved a sock in her mouth and wrapped it into place with gauze.

She struggled. She tried to use her power, begging Ti Malice for help. But her words were muffled by the gag, her mind dulled from all the medication.

She was being punished. Ti Malice would not help her.

The man grinned down at Cassandra.

"Not you, witch," he said, face still in shadow. "You stay. I hope you die. We have money on you, ya know. 'Will her body still be here after the storm blows through?' I put fifty on your bloated corpse still being handcuffed to this bed."

A crackle erupted from the overhead speaker. "Backup power will fail in thirty minutes. All staff are to leave now. Repeat, we are evacuating the building . . . ."

"Bye, witch," said the silhouette. "See you in hell!"

Cassandra's muffled screams and struggles against her restraints were absorbed by the howling winds of Katrina.

Curtis and Cassandra both staggered. Jeannine laughed.

"You tried to kill me with that storm, Mama, and it killed you instead! How perfect! There is that synchronicity you say you love so much." Jeannine raised the machete and continued to laugh. "I have more synchronicity coming soon, but I have to know: Why, if I were to be the next Cassandra, did you try to kill me?"

"Well, it should be obvious, child. If my master had awoken, there would have been no need for a new human advocate. Ti Malice would be free, and I would be serving at her side for all eternity. That is all I've ever wanted. But then you came along, and Ti Malice told me you would be the last, most powerful Cassandra."

The creature gave out a bitter little rasp.

"The power was mine!"

"And Jeannine was and is a threat to your power," said Curtis, regaining his own footing.

"Yes. But I miscalculated Ti Malice's love for me versus her love for her plan. With Katrina, I gave my master blood, buckets and buckets of blood. The waters were filled with the sacrifices I made to Ti Malice. But the lives the storm provided weren't enough. She wanted my daughter to finish what I'd brought about. I couldn't let my master dismiss me like that. I had to kill my daughter! And for that attempt, that conceit on my part, Ti Malice condemned me to rot in this place."

"Then why offer me your power back in that prison?"

"Nothing had worked. Ti Malice was still sleeping, though I could hear her whispers all throughout the bayou. She demanded to be set free, and I no longer had the strength to be of service to her. She needed a new advocate, a new Cassandra. It was time. I thought to try to end my suffering. To bestow upon you what my mother did for me, like her mother before."

"But you failed again," said Jeannine.

"I never thought you'd say no. Once you felt the power, how could you deny yourself what was offered? You are so damaged, my daughter. I thought seeking revenge would be worth the price of accepting the power."

"Revenge? Why would I want revenge? The men who abducted me, took me, are dead."

Again, Cassandra's wet laugh echoed around them.

"What about the white man who took you away from here? Do you remember that first night in his bed? All the soft words, soothing words he said as he lay on top of you . . ."

Jeannine took a step back, eyes wide, as if she'd been slapped.

Images, masquerading as memories, flooded into Jeannine's mind. Gifts. A new dress, a room filled with books and toys. A bed of her own to sleep in—the first time in six months. He told her how pretty she was. How smart. How proud he was that she made the decision to come with him to New York. To live in his home with all the floors and all the rooms.

He gave her wine at dinner. Every night. It always made her sleepy.

Her bed went untouched. She slept in his.

The sessions. The soothing words, the angry yelling. The manipulation.

"Just put it in your mouth," he whispered. "That's my girl . . ."

"I fucking knew it," snarled Curtis. "That sick, som'bitch. I fuckin' *knew* it."

Jeannine couldn't look at him. She knew, as an adult, how manipulative Stanley had been. But to a fourteen-year-old trauma survivor, Stanley had looked like a savior to her.

She tried to break away from him as she'd gotten older. But guilt prevented Jeannine from leaving Stanley. The bastard had saved her.

She loved and hated the man.

It was only when Curtis had called her, asked her for help after such a long silence between them, that she finally defied Stanley.

Jeannine's decision regarding the Louisiana bar exam was her first step away from the last of a long line of abusers.

She should have stayed with Curtis and told Stanley to fuck off all those years ago. But she hadn't been strong enough . . .

More wet laughter.

"You speak of my failure, daughter dear. It sounds like the pot calling the kettle a pedophile, I think."

Jeannine realized her mother had seen her thoughts. The skull with the ice-blue eyes was looking at Curtis now.

"What does she mean, Curtis?" Jeannine stared at him. *Not another betrayer . . .*

"She is full of shit," he growled. "I loved you then. Of course, I did," said Curtis. "I was planning on adopting you—we were. Georgina and I could never have our own children."

I hate you! Uncle Stanley, take me to New York! Take me away from this loser! I don't ever want to see him again!

The images echoed all around them.

"No, that never happened!" shouted Curtis, turning to glare at Cassandra's corpse. "Jeannine never said those things."

He turned back to the thing's daughter. "She's feeding us false memories, lies!"

"He's right, Mama. You're lying again."

"But he's a man," hissed Cassandra with a wet cackle. "I know how men think. Once you were in his home, he would have used you like those bayou rats did—"

Jeannine swung the machete, slicing Cassandra's head from her body in one quick blow.

Only Jeannine's heavy breathing and the buzzing of insects broke the silence.

She dropped the machete to the floor.

"Oh, God," said Jeannine, sinking to her knees. Curtis caught her and eased her to the ground.

"I wasn't expecting . . . I didn't know she was dead. And she always talked too much . . . like the snake whispering to Eve in the Garden of Eden . . . Oh, God, I cut off my mother's head."

"She wasn't your mother anymore," said Curtis quietly. "She was dead. For a long time, maybe."

"I never knew you wanted to adopt me," sobbed Jeannine.

"Georgina was the one to bring it up. She always wanted kids, but thought I'd never agree to adopt. Then she saw how much I cared for you. She knew, then, that it was time, because of who you were. Georgina felt so guilty for not stepping in sooner. She was afraid, I think. But your mother was right. I failed. It was too late. I let you go off with that som'bitch. I never even tried to fight him—Bernstein was causing so much trouble. I'm sorry I let him take you."

They were both on the floor now, among the weeds, bugs, and bones of Cassandra. They held each other, crying.

Finally, Jeannine gently pulled out of the embrace.

"Curtis," she said. "There is still something I don't understand. If she was dead this whole time, how did she speak to us? How did the power not just pass to me, or disappear altogether?"

There was a quiet scraping of metal on concrete.

"Because" said Easy Street, who was now holding Ms. Maxine as well as the ancient machete. "She wasn't running the show anymore. She was being punished the same way I've been punished for all these years."

"Nightmare," said Curtis.

"Correct. He knew Ti Malice would never give a man the power he craved. So, he kept your mother here, held her here, as his servant. Always the puppet master."

Curtis lunged toward Easy Street, but the ghoul dodged him. The former cop tripped over a root and hit the ground hard.

"Tsk. Still getting used to it, Mr. Curtis. It takes time," said Easy Street. Turning to Jeannine, he said, "Ms. Maxine and I have to thank you, Ms. Jeannine. Whatever you did to her case has been most helpful in hiding my thoughts. From you as well as Papa Nightmare. And, of course, from Mr. Curtis."

"I don't understand," said Jeannine.

"Neither do I," panted Curtis.

"Of course you do," said Easy. "Since the car accident, how have you felt?"

"I . . . fine. I've felt fine."

"Have you slept since then? Eaten?"

Curtis stared at him.

Jeannine brought her hand up to her mouth as realization dawned. "It's not possible," she said.

Curtis and Jeannine locked eyes.

"This blade," said Easy, "is very special. It not only cuts flesh and bone but severs magical ties. Like the ones that keep a ghost grounded in the real world."

Easy Street rammed the machete into Curtis's chest. It slipped between a couple of ribs, the tip ripping out of Curtis's back.

Jeannine screamed.

Curtis looked down at the blade in his chest, then back at Jeannine. "Huh. No blood," was all he said as he collapsed to the ground.

"My master asks that you do him the courtesy of rejoining him on his ship, Ms. Jeannine," said Easy Street as he pulled the machete out of Curtis's chest.

Curtis lay unmoving. Jeannine couldn't process what had happened. She was feeling nothing, thinking nothing.

She was like a radio tuned to a station that played only static.

"Shall we go?" asked the ghoul, pointing the ancient blade at Jeannine. "Your escort awaits, dig?"

Dozens of Civil War ghouls materialized silently from shadows, pointing their weapons at Jeannine.

TWENTY-FIVE

Bayou Cypress Pavilion for the Criminally Insane
New Orleans

THE CHEVY IMPALA pulled up behind the police SUV. Fernández shut off the engine, and he and the Golem listened to the *tink-tink* of the settling motor. Fernández tried Curtis's cell to no avail.

"What do you think?" asked Fernández, spitting out a wad of chewing tobacco.

"It's a Dismas Sheriff's vehicle, all right," said the Golem. "But if the Major were here, the place would be crawling with cops."

"Fair point. Let's go see if we can find the boss."

As they got out of the car and headed toward the old asylum, the Golem called a halt.

He was looking at the SUV.

"These things have GPS trackers in them, don't they?"

"Yeah," said Fernández. "Why?"

"Well, we don't want the Major or his goon squad showing up. Eventually, I assume they'll be looking for this piece of shit."

"True, but I have no idea how to disable the—"

The Golem picked up the truck and threw it into the bayou.

Fernández blinked. "You just like doing that, don't you?"

"You bet your ass," replied the Golem, and, looking at the foreboding overgrown entrance, he stroked his chin thoughtfully. "Better do this the quiet way."

"You threw a goddamn police SUV into a swamp. How was *that* the quiet way?"

"I mean from this point forward," said the Golem, as he bent down and began to sneak toward the entrance.

"Like that'll fucking work," muttered Fernández, but he followed his friend anyway.

The two men pulled up short when they eyed two skeletons standing watch at the front doors. The remains stood guard on either side of the entrance, facing each other.

"They didn't react to all our noise," Fernández said quietly. "More of Papa Nightmare's zonbi soldiers, ya think?"

"Want me to crush them into powder?" asked the Golem.

"Okay, you're scaring me with all this smashing and crushing shit, man," whispered Fernández. "Maybe we should find another way around."

"Maybe. But Jonesy might be in trouble and need our help. I say, frontal assault."

"No, I . . ."

The Golem had already moved. He reached the two sentries, who got off only a menacing hiss at the large man before he slammed their skulls together.

Their bones disintegrated.

The Golem motioned Fernández to follow as he disappeared into the ruins of the building.

"We're gonna have to talk, buddy," sighed Fernández, jogging to catch up. When he pulled up alongside the Golem, he said, "This place is a mess. No way anyone's living here."

"Try the boss's cell again."

Fernández took out Roo's phone and hit redial. They heard a distant buzzing.

"Boss?" called the Golem.

The phone rang out and Fernández pocketed it. "Yelling when there are obviously undead fucking monsters around probably isn't the smartest thing in the world," said Fernández.

"Fuck you very much for reminding me," said the Golem. "The buzzing came from there, I think." He pointed toward a corridor off the lobby.

"I think you're right. But where is that hissing coming from?"

Fernández and the Golem looked around and the long *hiss* grew louder. They both realized at the same time that the sound was coming from above.

The Golem shoved Fernández out of the way as a massive black snake, all undulating muscle with a body as thick as a grown man's thigh, unfurled itself from the exposed rafters and struck at the spot where the little man had been standing a second ago. Its mouth was filled with black, dripping fangs, long and lethal looking. Its head, the size of a large boar's, turned toward the Golem and hissed again.

The creature slithered from the ceiling, black glistening scales and muscle oozing to the floor, until, finally, a forked tail dropped with a splash into one of the stagnant pools of water. The creature was massive, perhaps thirty feet long, though it was hard to tell from the constantly moving coils that now separated the Golem from Fernández.

The creature reared up, its head eye level with the Golem. It swayed back and forth, looking at Charley, then down at Fernández. The snake opened its massive mouth, showing two rows of teeth, and spoke. "Insssolent thing of mud and magic it hissed. You denied me my sssnack!"

Fernández was dumbfounded, frozen in place. *Dios Mio! It talks!*

"Fernández!" snapped the Golem. "Shoot the big, scary, talking snake, please!"

The smaller man blinked once, then pointed his weapon. The heavy retorts of one of Roo's borrowed M-16s sent the massive reptile slithering across the debris-strewn floor faster than either man thought possible. The snake gave one last angry hiss, then plowed head-first into a pool of water near the old reception desk in what was left of the lobby.

Fernández slowly made his way toward the pool.

"If I see another forked tongue or tail; I'm using the 40-Mike-Mike on 'em," said Fernández.

"And blow your own ass into the bayou," replied the Golem.

"Fair point."

"Careful, buddy," said the Golem, as Fernández dipped one foot into the pool.

"Uh, Charley?" replied Fernández, as his foot touched the cement floor only an inch below the surface of the pool. "Somethin' ain't right."

Fernández had fully stepped into the pool now. There was no place for a snake of any size to hide in the water, let alone a creature the size he'd shot at.

"She long gone, boys," said a voice that echoed in the lobby all around Fernández and the Golem. "You scared her. I'd book it outta here if I was you. Terrible temper she has, dig?"

Fernández turned his weapon on the figure. A black man he'd never seen before stood at one of the hallway entrances, dressed in a grey suit, old-fashioned wide tie, and dark glasses. He carried a beat-up old hard canvas case—and a massive machete.

"Drop the knife, my man. Nice and slow," said Fernández, pointing his weapon at the man's chest.

"Oh, this?" asked the man, holding the weapon in front of his face. "I don't think so. My master likes to collect things, and this belongs to him. He let me borrow it for a spell, but it's done what it needed to."

The man pointed the blade at the Golem and smiled.

Fernández opened fire with a single controlled burst of three rounds.

Pieces of the rotted wall and rusted door frame behind the man flew in all directions.

"And here I thought we could be friends," the man said, his voice dripping with sarcasm. "Ol' Easy Street really don't like being shot at, dig?"

"Who?" said the Golem and Fernández together.

"Your boy. He down the corridor a-ways. He don't look so hot, if you ask me. But then again, being dead is like that. Bad for the skin."

"Oh, for fuck's sake. Another dead bastard," said the Golem. "You tell Papa Nightmare we already took care of some of his undead boys. We're ready for round two whenever he wants."

"I'll be sure to tell him," said Easy Street. "But you

might want to be careful with the big guns, boy. Papa Nightmare has a guest with him on board and she won't react well to bullets."

Easy Street saluted the men with his machete, then faded into nothing, a faint wisp of black smoke curling up from where the ghost had stood.

"I've about had my fill of this voodoo undead bullshit," said Fernández. "Let's go find the boss and figure out our next steps."

They found him less than a minute later, crumpled in a heap on the floor.

"Oh, fuck, Jonesy. That rat bastard wasn't lying," said Fernández, kneeling beside him.

The Golem growled, a sound from deep in his chest so low that it was felt rather than heard.

"Can you carry him?" asked Fernández.

"Yes. Where do you want me to take him?"

"Back to the car. We'll figure out the rest when—"

"Is that rat bastard gone?" asked Curtis.

"Holy fucking shit!" sputtered the smaller man, falling backward, his weapon clattering to the floor.

"You don't think I'd let a dead musician with a machete, or a stupid car accident stop me, do you?"

The Golem and Fernández stared wide-eyed as Curtis stood. He then held out his hand to help up Fernández.

Fernández wouldn't take it. He was still in shock.

"That voodoo som'bitch and his bitch-Loa are about to usher in the end of our world," Curtis said. "So, close your mouths, wipe that the bug-eyed look off your faces, and let's get moving. I don't know where Nightmare has taken Jeannine, but I know of someone who might be able to tell us."

TWENTY-SIX

The Sultana

S HE WOKE TO find her leg gone.
This time, her captors had removed her prosthetic before chaining her to a post. She wasn't in a cramped stateroom this time. She was below deck in a wide-open space, posts reaching from floor to ceiling, spaced every ten feet or so. The smell of the bayou was stronger here than it had been elsewhere on the cursed ship. A single oil lantern burned with a greenish-white glow, making her large prison—perhaps the old ballroom, she thought—look as though it was covered in moss and mildew. A constant dripping behind her began to take on a life of its own. Jeannine tried to ignore the rhythmic splashing, but despite her attempts, her mind counted the splashes. One. Two. Twenty. A hundred.

Someone, or something, coughed—a wet sound, perfectly matching her prison's rhythm.

"This must be the *Sultana,*" said a deep voice from behind her.

She couldn't believe it.

"Curtis?" she asked, voice cracking.

"Hiya, J," said the same voice.

Tears welled in her eyes. "You're dead. That jazzman killed you."

214

"Yeah," said Curtis. "I'm still trying to understand it all. Apparently, I died when I wrecked my car. Twenty-twenty hindsight—I'd wondered why all my pain had gone away. Guess I know why, now."

"I'm so sorry," she began.

"Don't be," he said. "I played the game and lost. It was bound to happen someday. I just wish "someday" was a bit later."

"I don't understand why he didn't kill me, too."

"You're too important for his plans." Jones coughed again, a hacking, musical sound.

"If you weren't already dead, I'd tell you to get that checked," replied Jeannine.

They both laughed.

"Nightmare must have grabbed my soul at the same time he grabbed you. I'm actually thankful he did. Gives me a chance to talk to you one last time," said Curtis. "There are a couple of things I wanted to say to you, but never had the courage to do so when I was alive. And now—courage doesn't matter anymore."

"What is it?"

"You know we were gonna adopt you—my wife and I."

"Georgina?"

"Yeah, Georgina and I decided it was the right thing. But while who you were and what your situation was at the time was reason enough to take you in, there was another reason."

"You don't have to tell me any of this."

"Let me finish, J. I ever tell you how I met my late wife?"

"I don't think so. After Stanley took me to New York, we never really had a chance to tell stories."

"I served with her brother. We were in N'Orleans on leave one spring and he hooked up with a singer while I was hooking up with his sister."

He paused as the *Sultana* creaked and the lantern shifted.

"Georgina's brother. He hooked up—with my mama." Jeannine said it as a fact. There was no question in her voice. As soon as Curtis had said "singer," she knew.

"Yes."

"So, I'm your niece."

"Yes."

"He was so excited to hear about your mama's pregnancy. He got the letter when we were in Iraq "peace-keeping" after the first Gulf War. The next day he was killed."

"That's why I never knew him. Why didn't you tell me before?"

"I made a promise to your mother. See, he died before you were born, dig?"

"I . . . what did you say?"

A laugh—a deep, menacing sound—danced around them.

"Motherfucker," hissed Jeannine.

The chains behind her clinked and shifted. A man appeared—it was Easy Street, wearing a wide toothy grin. He held his saxophone case close, and the ancient machete hung off his belt in a makeshift loop made of his silk necktie.

"We learn so much from the dead," said Papa Nightmare as he walked into Jeannine's prison. "I have always loved to hear their stories." Papa Nightmare turned to Easy Street. "Jazzman, I have one last task for you, and our path will be clear."

"I'm going to end you both, you know that," said Jeannine through gritted teeth.

Papa Nightmare turned back to Jeannine with a laugh. "You have a lot of spunk, girl. Ti Malice will appreciate that."

Jeannine, angry tears streaming down both cheeks, looked at Papa Nightmare with hatred. "What do you mean, motherfucker?"

"My lord," came an unfamiliar voice from the doorway. "We are nearing the shrine."

Papa Nightmare nodded, not taking his eyes off Jeannine. He squatted down to her eye level.

"The insolence in that look. Tsk," he said. "Maybe you are not quite ready to meet your destiny. Perhaps, one more reminder of my power, the power of the Loa, will help you see your place in the world."

She was naked with both the men in her. The pain was something she'd learned to push aside. And when she did, they'd stopped taking turns and abused her together. So, she would go to the place in her mind that had appeared that first time.

Water surrounded her. Cypress trees grew from the bayou, and great birds called to her. The sights and sounds were so familiar. She felt like the birds were welcoming her back.

In her fantasy, she floated on top of the pool, the scent of the water lotus calmed her, reminded her of how her mother smelled before the bad times. Happiness enveloped her and the sun, while shining as bright as it always did in Louisiana, was not too hot nor was the air too humid.

It was perfection.

"You are back, little one," said a gentle woman's voice.

From the depths, a woman appeared. She rose from the bayou, held aloft like Venus ascending in that old painting. The woman had hair the color and texture of the surrounding vines, and a smile as bright and warm as the sun. She was radiant, the water of the bayou adding an ethereal quality and luminescence to her skin.

"A goddess," said Jeannine breathlessly.

The goddess's eyes were closed. Yet, the woman of the bayou gave the impression she could see the teenager. She smiled down to her, and the girl smiled back.

"Yes, fanm ki gen bon konprann, wise lady, I have returned," said Jeannine. "Tell me another story—of ancient heroes and glorious battles!"

The woman of the bayou laughed. Her laugh sounded of wind chimes and summer rain.

"Why should I do this for you?" asked the lady. It was their private game. Jeannine would beg to hear the stories and the wise one would pretend to protest.

"Because they give me hope," said Jeannine, matching the lady's smile.

"Hope? Shall I tell you a story of hope? Of your mother, Cassandra, perhaps?"

Jeannine frowned. The tinkling wind chimes turned discordant, as the sound of grunting men echoed between the notes.

"No. My mother isn't hope. She is death." replied Jeannine. "Tell me of the old world and how the new will be made old once again."

The goddess's smile never faded as she cocked her

head to one side. The crystalline melody returned to harmony as the sounds of the men faded.

"Do not despair, little one. Your suffering is almost at an end. You must suffer before you can come be with me in this place, yes? I have told you all this before."

But the spell was broken for Jeannine.

"My leg hurts."

"I know," said the lady. "A little while longer. Someone comes to help you. They will be here soon."

"The men hurt me. Over and over."

"Focus on the stories," said the lady, her voice turning cold, as Jeannine shivered, a chill enveloping her.

Two loud reports snapped Jeannine back into the stinking mud room that was her prison. The two men weren't grunting anymore. They weren't even breathing.

A man with thick glasses stood there holding a gun. Round red holes adorned the men's heads—one each.

"Your mother sent me," said the man with the glasses. "My name is Charley."

He dropped rags at her feet.

"I heard your cries, child. But I cannot take you. That is the deal. You must find your way out by yourself. Dress, then go. Now. Head away from the sun and you will find the one to help you."

"Thank you," was all the young Jeannine could croak.

The man sank into the mud of the bayou, gun slipping from him with a soft splash.

Jeannine was alone with two dead men.

She looked at them dispassionately, satisfied at their fate. Then, without dressing, she began to walk.

Right foot, left foot drag . . .

❧

On the *Sultana*, Jeannine came out of her dream, lying on her side on the deck, shivering.

Papa Nightmare squatted down close to her and whispered, his lips brushing her ear, "You grow strong, little *plaçage*. But you are not strong enough. We have arrived at my lady's resting place. Ti Malice is looking forward to seeing you again."

TWENTY-SEVEN

The Bunker

THEY WERE TEN MINUTES from Curtis's place when the Golem finally spoke. "So, tell me again, how many times have you died?"

Curtis sighed. "Twice. The machete was number two. The car accident the other day was the first—I think."

"I don't believe this," grumbled Charley, shaking his head. "You *think* that was the first?"

"You're one to talk," said Curtis, frowning. "I don't claim to understand it. All I can tell you is that when I climbed out of the car, I felt no pain. *Nothing*, from any of my injuries in the crash—no pain at all. Not even my knees, which I've been bitching about since the war."

"What's, uh, keeping you here?" asked the Golem. "I know Roo brought me back using some of his voodoo stuff. But he's dead. I mean *dead*-dead. No one brought you back."

Curtis didn't speak for a minute or two, a faraway look to his eyes.

"That's a good question," he said slowly. "I know . . . there is a purpose to my being here. And before you ask, no, I don't know what it is. I somehow just *know*." He looked at Charley. "Maybe it's something like what's holding Easy Street here. Or Cassandra."

"Does that mean you are fucking working for that Voodoo bastard?" rumbled the Golem, shifting in the back of their borrowed ride.

Curtis smiled at that. "No, big fella. That's one thing I'm sure of. I feel *hatred* toward that som'bitch Nightmare. My honest guess? It's Jeannine, I think. Somehow, she's been doing this."

"She didn't know you were in an accident until the Major told her," said Fernández.

"I don't know. *You* explain it, then."

Fernández snorted. "I'm the only one in this car who's properly alive, *hombre*. I'm neither spirit nor clay."

The Golem remained silent and continued to brood in the back seat.

"We're here," said Fernández.

They came to a spot in the road where the thick grouping of trees parted, revealing a deeply rutted dirt road. They slowed and turned onto the unmarked road. The car bottomed out with a teeth-jarring clunk, and more than once the Golem slammed his head into the roof of the car. Before long, they reached a fork in the road. The road to the right was as worn as the road on which they'd entered the property. The left fork was more overgrown.

"Which way, boss?" asked Fernández.

"The main road to my trailer curves off to the right," replied Curtis. "The bunker is left."

Fernández nodded and the car began to roll slowly toward the left fork when Curtis asked him to stop.

A hundred yards to the right, Curtis saw a pile of

scorched debris fronted by yellow "Police Line Do Not Cross" tape.

The debris was all that was left of Curtis's home.

Curtis gave a sad-sounding little whistle. "You guys really cooked the place."

"You told us to," said the Golem, sounding resentful.

Curtis nodded. "I did. Just . . . a lot of memories went up in smoke, ya know? I need to go in there when we're done. I want to check to see if there is anything you guys missed."

Fernández turned in his seat to look at Curtis. "You mean, like a journal?"

The Golem glanced at Fernández, then turned his gaze toward Curtis, waiting for his answer.

Curtis grunted. "In the air vent?"

"Yeah. Roo found it. Said it was an "interesting read." Haven't gotten to it myself yet."

"Where is it?" asked Curtis quietly.

"Some place safe. Wanna give us a preview of what the Golem and I will find in it?"

"Later. I promise," said Curtis. "After we get Jeannine back. You should hear everything that's in it."

Fernández looked over to the Golem, who nodded.

"Okay, then," said Fernández, taking his foot off the brake.

Two hundred yards later, they came to a copse of trees. For most people, a first glance would have told them nothing out of the ordinary was present.

The ex-Rangers recognized a camouflaged bunker when they saw it.

"I wonder where they hid the ambulance?" mused Fernández.

"There's a broken-down barn a half mile up the road," said Curtis. "I'll bet they put it there."

The car rolled to a stop near the bunker, and Fernández turned off the engine. An uncomfortable silence followed.

"Well," said Curtis. "Let's go see if our resident PhD can tell us how to find Jeannine."

❧

"He's not doin' so well," said the man Curtis called "Legs." "We've given him a cocktail of morphine and Fentanyl to keep him under. But my supplies are running low."

They were in a large cement room, similar in size to Roo's storage unit. One corner had been sectioned off with plastic. In a hospital bed lay an unconscious Dr. Stanley Bernstein connected to an IV and vital sign monitor secured next to the bed. The readings on the monitor were all low and the unit beeped menacingly every thirty seconds.

Curtis didn't care.

"Wake him," said Curtis.

Legs shook his head. "Boss . . . " he began to protest, but Curtis cut him short.

"Do it. Now."

The EMT shrugged and adjusted the flow of the unconscious man's IV medications. He then pulled a syringe of some clear liquid from a drawer next to the bed and injected the fluid into a spare port on the IV.

"I've reduced the Fentanyl and administered some naloxone. He'll hopefully wake up in an hour or so," said Legs.

"Hopefully?" asked Curtis.

"Shit, boss," said Harve, "we had to give him a

pretty strong dose to keep him under. Frankly, he might not be able to answer you—ever. We have him on a large dose of antibiotics to stem infection, and we've field dressed his abrasions, gashes, and broken bones as best we can. The bottom line is this man will die if we don't get him to something better than a makeshift field hospital."

"I don't give a shit," replied Curtis. "Just wake him up. We need to question him."

The tension in the room was as thick as the fog of the bayou. Legs cleared his throat.

"Like I said . . . it will take time."

Curtis nodded. Then added suddenly, "I'm going for a walk." He spun on his heels and made his way up the stairs of the bunker.

"Go with him," Curtis heard Fernández say to the Golem.

The ghost and the Golem walked toward the burned-out wreckage of Curtis's home. His life, the life he'd made with Georgina—the spare room he and his wife had prepared for Jeannine so long ago yet couldn't bring themselves to remodel after she left with Bernstein—all gone.

"Jonesy," said the Golem, after they both had scrounged around the wreckage in silence for three-quarters of an hour. "What's in the journal?"

"Notes. On everything," he said.

"What do you mean, 'everything'?"

Curtis sighed. He wanted to wait, to tell everyone together. But here, in full view of the wreckage his life had become . . .

Perhaps being dead is a blessing.

The words flowed from the ghost.

"At first I was documenting the Major and his

rotten activities and businesses. Then I expanded to include Nightmare's criminal empire. That lead to what Roo thought was "interesting" reading."

"Did you document our jobs?" asked the Golem quietly.

Curtis looked up at the big man. After a few seconds of silence, Charley had his answer. His shoulders sagged and he looked away from Curtis.

"Jesus, Roo made a huge new body for you, didn't he?" Curtis remarked.

"Jonesy . . . "

The ghost looked away before answering the Golem's question. "Yes, I documented everything."

"For fuck's sake, why? Not that it really matters to me. There isn't a prison that could hold me and, like you, I'm dead. At least on paper. But Fernández . . . "

"Before I began to document our activities," said Curtis, "I negotiated a "get out of jail free" card for all of us."

"With who? Who is the journal for?"

"Boss!" called out Fernández, who'd followed them to the ruined double-wide. "Bernstein's awake."

❧

Bernstein looked shrunken in his bed. His eyes were open wide and glassy.

"I'm going to die," whimpered the som'bitch.

"Probably," said Curtis. "You get used to it."

"Oh, God," sobbed Bernstein, fat tears leaking down his cheeks. "Where am I?"

"Focus, Bernstein," said Curtis, leaning over Bernstein. "Nightmare. How do we get to him?"

"Papa Nightmare?" slurred Bernstein between sobs. "I don't know. Papa Nightmare? Big black guy?"

"He's still loopy from the Fentanyl," said Legs. "Might be days before he's coherent enough to answer your questions with any detail, boss."

"The Major!" said Bernstein. "Papa Nightmare and the Major will help me, get me a doctor . . . "

Curtis tried not to throttle the man in frustration.

"What's Nightmare's connection to the Loa?" asked Curtis.

At this question, Bernstein's swollen, bloodshot eyes turned from Curtis to stare at a blank spot on the wall.

"C'mon, you som'bitch," said Curtis. "Give us something and we'll get you to a hospital."

"Of course, you won't," said Bernstein, giving a laugh that turned into a cough. "You have to kill me—because as soon as I get to a hospital, I'll have every cop and Fed in Louisiana hunting you all down. You *know* I will."

Bernstein and Curtis glared at one another.

"If you ever cared for her at all, you'll give me something," said Curtis.

Bernstein continued to look at Curtis for a couple of heartbeats, then turned away.

"C'mon, you cocksucker," snarled Curtis. This time, he grabbed Bernstein by the neck.

"Jonesy, no!" said Fernández. He grabbed his boss and tried to pull him off Bernstein to no avail.

The Golem stepped in, putting a gentle hand on Curtis's shoulder, and said, "Think of Jeannine."

Curtis let go and Bernstein fell back on the bed, gasping for air.

"I swear to God I'm gonna kill him before this is all over," snarled Jones.

"I'll take care of that for you, Mr. Curtis, dig?"

They all spun around in time to see Easy Street, machete in both hands, rush at them. Legs was nearly cut in half, spilling his guts all over the floor with a scream. Harve lost the top of his head and fell to the ground, leaking brains that mixed with Legs' spilled organs.

The Golem got a hand on the dead jazzman, but Easy tossed him aside like the clay man was a rag doll.

Easy plunged the blade into the shrink's chest before anyone else could intercept him.

"Papa Nightmare sends his best," said Easy Street, twisting the blade.

Curtis punched the ghost in the mouth, knocking his sunglasses away. Easy Street fell to the ground. He gazed up at Curtis with a stunned look on his eyeless face.

"Hello, you little bitch," said Curtis.

Curtis pulled the machete out of the dead psychologist's chest and pointed it at the jazzman. "As I understand it, this blade will kill you once and for all. If you don't want to find out how much hotter hell is compared to Louisiana, you'll take me to see Papa Nightmare right now."

TWENTY-EIGHT

The Sultana

"**M**Y MOTHER WAS *trying to kill me,*" she thought.

Jeannine was back on Toulouse Street in the last place she'd lived with her mother. She knew this was another of Papa Nightmare's visions, but she could do little to stop it from playing out.

The hairs on her arms stood straight up. Danger! Danger was approaching!

She ducked as the massive blade swung, slicing through air where her neck had been a split second before. Jeannine screamed as she scrambled away from her attacker.

"You won't betray me! Or steal my power! I'll kill you first!" screamed her mother.

Jeannine ran.

In her panic, she ran the wrong way. Instead of running out the front door, Jeannine turned to the stairs and ran to her room.

Her mother followed.

Jeannine locked the door. She ran to the windows—the ones her mother said never to open. She tried to move the paint-chipped wooden frames, first hammering at them with her hands, then

229

throwing her entire body at the window. A tree outside stood within reach if only the windows would open.

But the glass wouldn't break.

There was a gentle knocking at the door.

"Dear-heart, open the door. It's Mama."

There was a loud thunk *as something metallic was driven into the door.*

Her mother was trying to break it down.

"You know this is the way it has to be," called her mother's voice. "You are too strong, Dear-heart. You see that, don't you? I am Cassandra! Ti Malice loves me not *you. You threaten us, so you have to die. Open the door and I promise it will be quick."*

Mama sounded normal, like herself, but . . .

Another thunk, and a piece of wood chipped off into Jeannine's room.

. . . why was she doing this? She sounded sweet and loving, yet she was destroying the door to get to Jeannine. Why?

Jeannine wrapped her arms around herself, rocking in place. She had no idea what to do. There was no one to call. No one to save her.

"Mama! Why are you doing this?"

"You know why, Dear-heart," answered her mother. "One slice. It will be clean. No one will even see the gash as you lay in your coffin. I'll put that pretty lavender dress with the high neck on you. No one will see and you'll look so peaceful."

Thunk!

Jeannine screamed.

More wood fell from the door.

One ice-blue eye looked in at her now.

"Mama loves you," the eye said. "It will be quick.

I'll drink your blood and have the power I need to wake Ti Malice. It's perfect! With your blood, we'll be together. Let me in, let me have your blood."

Thunk!

Jeannine closed her eyes. She shut them so tight she saw stars against a black field of nothingness.

"Please," she thought. "Please, somebody help me."

Jeannine heard music. It sounded like chimes, tinkling in a light summer breeze. She smelled fragrant, sweet iris flowers and phlox. The earthier scents, the cypress trees, and the bayou. She saw a woman, floating in water, wrapped in vines and roots.

"St. Louis No. 1," she whispered. "You can do it. Concentrate."

Her mother hacked at the old door again and again until a hole formed that would fit her hand and arm. She reached in and unlocked the door.

"Now, my beautiful daughter, we will be together! We will serve Ti Malice . . . Malice."

St. Louis No. 1. The cemetery across the street.

Jeannine focused on it, focused on the raised tombs and mausoleums. Focused on the dead.

She called to them—and they answered.

Her mother took but a single step into the room, when she was stopped by a hand on her ankle. Looking down, Cassandra screamed, "No! She cannot! I will not allow it! Ti Malice! Hear me!"

"Ti Malice speaks to me, now, Mama," answered Jeannine in a singsong voice.

Cassandra screamed again.

Skeletons covered in muck and worse crawled all over Jeannine's mother. Cassandra hacked at them with the machete she'd used on the door. She called Ti Malice's name over and over as she sliced at bones and rotting flesh. Other dead things formed a wall of skeletons between Cassandra and Jeannine. Protecting Jeannine from her mother's onslaught.

"Ti Malice! Ti Malice!" screamed her mother. The machete sliced at one of the dead, striking Jeannine's arm. Blood poured from her, pooling on the bed and the ground.

"Yes! Thank you, Ti Malice . . . Malice . . . " Cassandra sang in triumph. She dove to the ground to lap up the blood, but Jeannine touched her mother's head.

Power.

Jeannine felt as though electricity coursed through every nerve ending in her body. She screamed. Cassandra screamed.

The skeletal wall fell to the floor, unmoving.

Blood was everywhere.

The night returned to uneasy soundlessness. Except for her mother's whispers.

"Malice-malice-malice . . . "

Jeannine looked around the room and smiled, her now ice-blue eyes taking in the details.

"I have your mind now, Mother. And it's glorious!"

⚜

"Do you understand yet, little *plaçage*?" said Nightmare. He loomed over Jeannine. She sat, still chained to the *Sultana,* still below the main deck in what had been the massive ballroom.

She spat at Papa Nightmare.

His face contorted into fury as he wiped the spittle from his cheek.

For a moment, Jeannine thought he would strike her. Maybe even kill her. But the Voudon priest wrestled his seething emotions. A smile reappeared on his face.

"Do you see the beauty of your suffering? No? Perhaps another trip through your memories, then."

It was the middle of the night and she was the only one in Vanderbilt Hall at the NYU law library studying for the New Orleans bar exam. In an annex off the main floor, she sat in an alcove that provided her with quiet seclusion during busy times in the library. She'd chosen this place more out of habit, since it was the night before graduation and all the other students were out partying.

Over the years, Jeannine had become friendly with the guards who worked in Vanderbilt Hall. The only one on duty this evening was old man Petersen. His only complaint to Jeannine about her wanting to use the library this late was that she'd woken him from an awesome dream that involved Jennifer Aniston.

Men.

"Hey Jeannie, what are you up to?"

Jeannine looked up from her books in surprise. It was Steve Ballintyne, a fellow law student and Jeannine's on again, off again lover. One look at his eyes, and Jeannine knew he was looking for the relationship to be "on" again.

"Hey," she said. "Cramming for the bar. You studying, too?"

"Nah," he said, pulling out the chair next to her. "I'm ready. I'll be joining my dad's firm downtown after graduation."

He placed a hand on her thigh.

"Must be nice to have Daddy's influence watching over your career," she said, pointedly removing his hand. "I, on the other hand, have to study. So, unless you're going to crack open a book with me, if you don't mind . . . "

"But I do mind," he said, his hand back on her thigh and climbing. He leaned in close. "I thought we both could use a little R&R," he whispered.

She smelled the bourbon on his breath.

She forcibly removed his hand again. "I said no, motherfucker. Now get away from me—"

He hit her.

Jeannine saw stars as she toppled to the floor.

Steve was on top of her. He clawed at her blouse, tearing at the buttons, shredding the thin fabric with his nails.

"Motherfucker, is it?" he snarled. He punched her in the mouth with a closed fist, her lip splitting and splattering them both with blood. The stars swam around her, and she nearly blacked out. He easily blocked her attempts to hit back.

"How about just fucker? As I remember, you liked it when I played rough." He ripped the last bits of her blouse off and began pulling at her bra. "I think you like it hard and rough. Must remind you of those good ole' boys who held you hostage in Louisiana, was it?"

Jeannine's arms turned to dead weight. She was half-unconscious, and he was so much stronger. Her mind screamed as she heard his laughter, and the laughter of the two filthy bayou rats . . .

⚜

Papa Nightmare paced around Jeannine like a cat toying with a mouse. He stood behind her now, and close. She smelled his putrid breath, smelled his sweat.

"What happened next, girl?" purred Papa Nightmare into her ear. "You don't remember, do you? Let me tell you the rest of the story myself."

Across from your law library was Washington Square park—a beautiful New York City park with elm trees, highlighted by the circular fountain in the middle and the Washington Square Arch near the Fifth Avenue entrance. You remember it, yes?

The park, a tourist attraction, and a place for owners to run their dogs, was once a potter's field for indigent, yellow fever victims and, as legend had it, home of an ancient elm tree that served as gallows. That, you didn't know, little plaçage, did you? But some place, deep down, you must have sensed it.

As the one you knew as Steve Ballintyne attacked you again and again, a rumble was heard in the park. The great Arch cracked. The fountain split in two, spilling filthy water over the meticulously landscaped flower beds.

The park had been built over the tombs of some 20,000 men, women, and children. You sensed them, didn't you?

The dead rose up that night—called to protect their mistress. Called by you.

The poor security guard at the desk of the library—what did you say his name was? Old man Petersen?—he never stood a chance as the hoard of bones broke into the library and swarmed around and over him, smothering the old man at his desk. He was a friend of yours, and you killed him to save yourself.

That man pulling down your pants, calling you names and continuing to hit you. He was about to fuck you, wasn't he, little plaçage, when the dead pulled him off you. When you finally came to your senses, you found yourself partially naked, surrounded by dirt and old bones—and a red smear.

"Leave," whispered a voice. "Leave now, they'll never know you were here."

You listened to Ti Malice and fled . . .

Jeannine jerked from the vision, once again back on the *Sultana*.

"You don't remember that last bit, do you?" said Papa Nightmare. "The New York papers had a field day with the story. 'Horror in the Stacks' was the headline. They said they found books on New Orleans state law strewn around the remains. Which, of course, told us all who was responsible."

Papa Nightmare finally walked into Jeannine's line of sight.

"You get it now, little *plaçage*, don't you?"

"What . . . what am I supposed to get?"

"All these years—you've been the Cassandra the entire time. You took your mother's place the night you defeated her, taking her mind, taking her *power*. It has been all you ever since. Not a bag of rotting bones in a washed-out hospital, nor a specter whispering to you on the breeze. It's you. And now it's time for you to make one last sacrifice for Ti Malice.

Time for you to end, Cassandra. Time for Ti Malice to wake at last."

He opened a door on the deck of the *Sultana*'s ball room. Beyond it, all Jeannine saw was an empty blackness.

"Allow me to make the introduction."

TWENTY-NINE

The Sultana

HELLO, CHILD.
"Where am I?" asked Jeannine.

Papa Nightmare was gone, the *Sultana* was gone. Jeannine stood in a place of complete darkness. It was then she noticed she was standing on two good legs.

Scents of cypress and lotus filled her nostrils. The air around her felt damp. Goose flesh rose up on her skin. Life and death fought for the attention of her senses as the darkness changed, morphed. She stood at the edge of the water, barefoot and clothed in a dress made of vines and branches. She walked along the edge of the bayou. Near her feet, alligator eggs hatched, tadpoles swam, and a crane flew for the first time. She saw rotting trees and the corpse of a boar being reclaimed by the bayou.

A large black snake slithered up to her, but Cassandra wasn't afraid.

We finally meet face to face, child. Centuries of planning and dining on dead things has led us to the end. The snake's tongue flickered in time with the words that appeared in Jeannine's head.

"My name is Jeannine," she said. Her mouth never moved either.

That hasn't been your name in a long time, child. Since your mother tried to ruin my plans. Papa Nightmare kept her alive for me to explain the error of her ways to her. As did you.

"I don't understand."

I do not expect you to, child. Understanding is not required. Only obedience and power matter. Your mother failed me. She almost ruined everything. But in her arrogance, her mistake made you, and I could not be more pleased with the result.

"Why am I here?"

To return to me the gift I loaned. While I slept, only a small part of me remained conscious of the world of humans. A world your kind has nearly destroyed. But I've grown strong and I will return this world to the animals and plants that live, thrive, and die with my thoughts.

The snake, nearly thirty feet of undulating muscle, wrapped itself in a loose coil around Jeannine's leg and half of her torso.

And all I need is the power I gave to you and the Cassandras before you. I need that power returned so I can fully wake and restore the world.

"What if I don't want to return power to you? What if I want to keep it for myself?"

The snake let out a long hiss that sounded like laughter.

You have no choice, child. I am in your mind now, like you were in your mother's mind, like she in yours. My faithful servant Papa Nightmare can and will kill you if I allow it. The power would return to me then, but it would be damaged, corrupted. I might not be able to wake. But if my power is returned to me of your own free will? That will keep my essence pure and intact.

"You're afraid, Ti Malice. I can feel it. You are in my mind, that's true. But I'm in yours, as well. I can smell the fear coming from you. It smells of death and rotting things. Why is that, Ti Malice? Why are you afraid?"

The snake's coils began to tighten around Jeannine, pressure building from her toes to the bottom of her rib cage.

Insolence cannot be tolerated, child. You have one final purpose this day. To return what was given to you and the ones before you. Your purpose is done.

"You are a lying motherfucker," said Jeannine. "I can see your mind, snake. I can see you fear my ability to choose. To make my own decisions, just like my mother did when she tried to kill me. You fear I will keep your power, keeping you trapped and asleep forever."

The snake squeezed tighter.

Jeannine laughed. "You cannot harm me here. We are in *my* mind, asshole, and we'll play by *my* rules."

Jeannine waved a hand and the snake released her with an angry hiss.

This is your mind, yes, child. But while you are here with me, what is happening to your body, I wonder?

⚜

Jeannine came back to herself and opened her eyes to bedlam.

A dozen Civil War ghosts fought Charley Mouton, the Golem, and . . . *Curtis!*

The Golem was beating undead soldiers with the body of one of their own and Curtis was shooting as many as he could with his pistol. Easy Street lay near

Jeannine, spectral blood oozing from a third bullet hole in his head. A broken and trampled saxophone case and a flattened Ms. Maxine lay next to the machete she'd seen him use to stab Curtis.

But Curtis was here now.

Papa Nightmare screamed at his forces as more of the undead soldiers poured into the space. Bullets from different centuries flew around the room and splinters of wood and bits of undead soldiers sprayed everywhere, courtesy of the Golem. Jeannine crawled toward Easy and grabbed the machete. With a couple of hacks, she broke through the chains that held her to the post.

All she had to do now was stand.

Papa Nightmare had taken her prosthetic, so she used the ancient sword and the post to which she'd been chained to prop herself up. The Golem roared as he grabbed two more soldiers and smashed them against the wall. Curtis had stopped firing his gun— and was using the weapon as a club, beating the undead now swarming him.

But Charley and Curtis were fighting a losing battle of numbers.

Jeannine balanced herself on one leg. Papa Nightmare backed toward her as a hoard of grey and blue rushed at the clay man and the ghost. The Voodoo priest turned to look at Jeannine.

He had ice-blue eyes.

We have won! screamed Ti Malice using Papa Nightmare's voice. *Return my power and I will spare your friends. Do it now, Cassandra.*

"My name . . . is *Jeannine!*" she shouted back.

Years of abuse, of pain welled up inside of her. Wrapped around the anger was the love she felt for

Curtis. Her true family. She finally understood what had been obvious to others for so long.

And that pain, and her love, were stronger than anything else on that goddamn boat.

Jeannine leapt at Papa Nightmare using her one good leg and drove the machete through his open mouth and out the back of his skull.

The noise of battle ceased around them. The undead soldiers from long ago melted into the decking of the *Sultana*. The ship itself began to disintegrate as spectral planks gave way to rushing water.

"Go!" screamed Curtis.

The ghost ship rocked as its boilers exploded. With Papa Nightmare dead, there was nothing to hold the ghost ship together. Time was suddenly catching up with the old ship. The *Sultana* was reliving its death by fire from over a century ago.

"Go now!" screamed Curtis.

The main deck buckled and splintered as a massive fireball exploded from the engine room, hungrily consuming the ship's timbers, destroying everything in its path.

The Golem grabbed Jeannine and jumped off the dying ship into the water below.

Jeannine hit the surface, and everything went black.

She was in a featureless, dark room.

This time, it wasn't her mother tormenting her, or memories tearing at her.

Before her was the shape of a large vehicle, a car of some sort. She saw the flair of a cigarette and the silhouette of a young man leaning against the shadowy car.

Jeannine walked closer and saw that it was a young version of Curtis, wearing his cop uniform.

"Hey kid," he said, and took another drag.

"Hey," she responded, and walked over to him to match his pose, leaning against the car.

Jeannine saw that they were leaning on his classic Buick Grand National.

They stood in silence for what felt like an eternity. Finally, she broke the silence.

"I'm sorry," she said.

"Nah," he said, and dropped the butt on the ground, grinding it with his heel. "Don't be sorry. Be better. Be better than me."

"I don't know how," she said, amazed at her own honesty. "I don't even know how to be *me*."

"You'll learn. You are the smartest person I ever met. Even back when you were a teenager, you were smarter than me."

"I don't feel smarter," said Jeannine, looking out to the infinite blackness that surrounded them.

"Trust me, you are. You just need to act the part. "If ye have faith as a grain of mustard seed, ye shall say unto this mountain, remove hence to yonder place; and it shall remove; and nothing shall be impossible unto you." Matthew 12:20."

Jeannine snorted. "You quoting the Bible at me now?"

Curtis laughed, too. "You would've had a lot of that if you'd come to live with Georgina and me."

Jeannine's smile faded. "I'm sorry," was all she could think to say.

"Stop apologizing, kid. If anyone needs to

apologize, it's me. I should have told you the truth a long time ago."

Jeannine looked at Curtis, raising an eyebrow, waiting for an explanation.

"I knew your dad," he said. "I served with him. He was the reason I met Georgina. And the reason I should have taken you in from the get go. But . . . I was afraid. Afraid I wouldn't be good enough."

"I don't understand," said Jeannine.

Georgina's brother . . . he's your father. I am . . . was . . . your uncle."

Jeannine had a million and one questions, but something tugged at her, caused her to move away from Curtis.

"Find out who you really are!" he called. "Only then will we be able to speak again!"

The wind swirled around Jeannine, taking her away from Curtis.

Interstate 10 Eastbound

When Jeannine awoke, she was lying on the road, the same road she found herself on last time she escaped from the *Sultana*. But this time she wasn't alone.

The Golem was with her.

"What . . . what happened?" she asked.

"I think we won," said the Golem. "Let's get you out of the center of the road." He gently picked her up, carried her to an area of tall grass, and laid her down.

The wind whipped from the bayou as drops of rain splashed on them.

"S'only the wind," mumbled Jeannine. "The bayou isn't whispering to me anymore."

"Jeannine! Your eyes!" said the Golem.

"Huh?"

"Your eyes . . . they're brown!"

"Cool," she mumbled, as the blackness took her once more.

THIRTY

New Orleans

JEANNINE SPENT THE next week reading Curtis's journal while waiting on her new prosthetic. It wasn't like the countless and soulless briefs she'd studied for school and later for practice. Curtis wrote with passion. He documented what he saw and what he had uncovered for years. The shocking discovery was that his removal from the police force and his subsequent transition to crime had been sanctioned by his handlers: the FBI.

After two days of reading, she closed the journal on the last entry, a note to her, written with that same passion she'd never gotten the chance to really know. With tears in her eyes, she knew what had to be done next. Some loose ends needed to be sorted.

Curtis's land was hers now, and she would build a proper home there someday, but the bunker was comfortable enough for now. Until things were tied up, she actually felt safe there. A rare thing as of late.

The first call she made was to Fernández, who was busy poring over all of Roo's notes—scraps of paper and Post-its that had been haphazardly strewn about his workshop. Fernández had found a recipe for jambalaya mixed in with notes on golem creation, Voudon ceremonial details written on a used napkin that also noted the ingredients for a Marsala sauce.

"We still have some unfinished business," she said by way of a greeting when she called Fernández.

"The Golem and I were just discussing that," he replied.

"I assume Charley wants to smash pretty much everything," she said.

Fernández laughed. "Yes, especially the traitor and the Major." The humor left his voice as he said, "And he wants a proper funeral for Jonesy."

Jeannine swallowed hard, but her voice was strong and steady when she answered. "I have an idea about both, though the first part doesn't involve so much property damage and has the added benefits of being legal and currying favor with authority, leading to . . ."

"Let's hear it," said Fernández.

"Not over the phone. I'll meet you at the caretaker's cottage in a couple of hours."

"See you then," he said, and hung up.

Jeannine then made a second call that lasted the better part of an hour.

Greenwood Cemetery Caretaker's Cottage
New Orleans

"I don't like it at all," said Fernández, when Jeannine laid out her plan. The Golem growled in agreement.

As the Golem began to protest, Jeannine held up her hand and quieted them both with a look.

"It's not as satisfying as crushing their skulls, I get that," she said, nodding at the Golem. "But you guys have to think long term. My way is far better. Plus, based on what I read in Curtis's journal, I think we're fucked if we don't do it this way."

"Curtis was the thinker. That's why he was in charge," said Fernández.

"Well, isn't it good that I'm in charge now?" asked Jeannine with a smile.

"What?" said the Golem and Fernández together.

"You," said Jeannine, pointing her finger at Fernández. "You like shooting things and asking questions later."

He winked at her but didn't say anything.

"And you," she said, rounding on the Golem. "You use trucks as clubs to beat people. Neither of you are "thinkers." Curtis and Roo were the thinkers. They're both dead now. I'm the only one left to keep you motherfuckers out of trouble. Get me?"

Both men were smart enough not to argue the point.

FBI Field Office
New Orleans

The Louisiana FBI field office was not located in the capital city of Baton Rouge, but right in New Orleans on Leon C. Simon Boulevard. That had been the second call she'd made. It took some time to get to the agent in charge, but once Jeannine had gotten through to her and shared what she knew via the journal, she was invited to the downtown office the very next day.

Of course, Jeannine hadn't told Fernández and the Golem that the meeting she'd proposed to them had already been set. It was just another little white lie so the boys could feel they'd been consulted.

She pulled into the parking garage, went through the metal detector, and presented her identification. She was handed a badge and escorted to a small, windowless conference room. A very polite young man offered her coffee or water, and she equally politely declined. She waited for a quarter of an hour before the door opened and a middle-aged man entered the room.

He was handsome and rugged looking, with salt and pepper temples, glasses, and a nice light grey suit paired with a fashionable blue tie.

Jeannine stood, looking confused.

"Forgive me," said Jeannine. "I was expecting Special Agent Greene. Is she unavailable?"

"I'm afraid she is on assignment, Ms. LaRue. I'm Assistant Director Edwin Palmer." The man handed her a white rectangle with the FBI's logo on the back. "My card," he added.

Jeannine glanced at the card. "Boston office? You're a long way from home, Assistant Director."

"Shall we sit?" he said, ignoring the question in her voice.

They both sat. Jeannine noticed he was sizing her up. Not sexually, of course. That wasn't the behavior of someone who'd made Assistant Director.

He was sizing her up as an adversary.

She'd done this dance too many times in the past not to recognize the opening move of a chess match.

"To what do I owe the pleasure of an interview with a high-ranking member of the FBI?" asked Jeannine.

"Pleasure? Such an interesting word," said Palmer. "When you called about Curtis Jones and his journal, the mention of his name set off alarm bells in my office. I hopped on the first flight I could get out of Logan."

"That doesn't explain why you wanted to chat with me."

"Well, because he's a known associate of one Jeannine LaRue."

"I . . . what does the FBI want with *me*?"

"Want?" repeated Palmer in a way that reminded Jeannine of Stanley. "Nothing in particular. Just to speak with you. You are on a list that's been provided to us—the government—regarding individuals with, shall we say, specific talents? Individuals with potential."

"I can already tell you aren't going to elaborate on that, are you?"

Palmer smiled. "I'm afraid not. For the moment anyway."

"Who *are* you?"

"I run a major projects office for the FBI concerned with very special cases, and what Mr. Jones was working on for the Bureau overlapped between the local field office and my division."

"Major projects? Curtis Jones was investigating a crooked cop and a criminal empire run by a self-proclaimed Voodoo priest. Are you with the Criminal Investigative Division? I thought they were only interested in Eurasian organized crime?"

"You know a lot about us, Ms. LaRue. Perhaps you'd like to join the FBI?" he asked with a wry smile. "But, no, I'm not with CID. The late Mr. Jones was not just watching and reporting on the corruption of one of your local parish sheriff's offices. He was also reporting on strange phenomena in the New Orleans region. My office assigned him the armored car heist as part of ongoing investigations . . . "

"The way you said "phenomena" makes me think of *The X-Files* or *Fringe*."

"Never saw either show. But tell me, Ms. LaRue," said Palmer, leaning forward. "What do you know about *magic*?"

Jeannine sat back in her chair, stunned. "Well, Assistant Director, that's a big ask, to be sure. As an officer of the court, I would be happy to discuss what I've learned and read in Curtis's journal."

Palmer squinted over his glasses at Jeannine. "Your tone implies a 'but.'"

She smiled. "How very perceptive. *But* first I need three favors from the FBI."

Palmer frowned. "I'm not sure I can grant any favors, Counselor."

"Since you flew all the way here on a moment's notice to meet with me face to face, I feel I'm in a pretty good negotiating position. And please don't lead off with all the bluster about arresting me and/or my friends or trying to appeal to my sense of patriotism. You want something from me—and it's important. It's written all over your face. So, let's deal."

Palmer put his pen on the table, leaned back in his chair, and removed his glasses.

Typical, she thought. But your body language doomed the rest of your chess pieces, Assistant Director.

"Oh, c'mon, Palmer. I'll show you mine if you show me yours," said Jeannine out loud.

Palmers sighed. "Ask me your favors, and I'll see what I can do."

With negotiations completed and an agreement to speak again when the Assistant Director fulfilled his promises, Jeannine left the FBI field office. Palmer, deep in thought, watched her go.

After the woman got into her car and drove off, he pulled out his mobile and dialed a number.

"Yes, Ms. Engel, I think you and the Monsignor were right. Ms. LaRue's the one we've been looking for. I'll be meeting up with her again in the coming days. I'll circle back with you then."

Palmer ended the connection.

He stood in the lobby, watching Jeannine's now empty parking space for nearly thirty minutes before dialing his team lead.

Arrangements needed to be made.

Bourbon Street
New Orleans

"I still think I should go in there and rip his traitorous head off," groused the Golem as they sat in a car a block from Gallow's restaurant.

"I'm sure you do," said Fernández. "Trust me, this is going to hurt him for a very long time."

Not five minutes later, a half-dozen unmarked cars roared up to Gallow's restaurant. A dozen agents stormed in, right at the onset of the dinner rush. Customers came out in droves, and Gallow was brought out in handcuffs as an FBI van pulled up.

When he happened to glance down the road, the Golem and Fernández flashed him stunning smiles and wiggled their fingers at him.

Gallow turned beet-red and hung his head in defeat.

"Okay, you were right. That was pretty sweet," said the Golem, as he used his new smartphone to take a picture of the restaurateur in handcuffs. "I just wish Jeannine had been here to see it. She made this happen after all."

"Oh, trust me, Charley. She's enjoying herself all fine and dandy-like. This was an appetizer. She's already enjoying the main course," Fernández said as he put the car into drive.

St. Dismas Sheriff's Office

"Meow!"

Ollie the three-legged cat sat on the dash of Jeannine's rental car. She'd gone back to Roo's old place to find the cat pawing at a human rib bone it had retrieved when Nightmare's undead attacked the place. She decided to adopt the animal right there.

She and the cat sat in a parking lot at the top of a grade that overlooked the St. Dismas Sheriff's headquarters. The FBI were already swarming the building when she'd pulled into a prime spot. Palmer had texted her a summary—twenty dirty cops, including the Major, had been handcuffed and loaded into a large, armored paddy wagon. The "good" cops had been meticulously identified by Curtis, and they had been instrumental in rounding up the bad eggs for the FBI. Good women and men were now in charge of the parish's police force.

The old adage "follow the money" had paid off. Curtis's notes, along with Jeannine's testimony, had opened the door enough for the FBI's financial forensics team to completely unravel the Major's underhanded business dealings.

Now, the team below were wrapping up, and Jeannine had a flight to catch.

"C'mon, Ollie. It's time to head north to say goodbye."

The cat stretched, then jumped down onto the passenger seat, eyeing Jeannine as if to say, "Why aren't we moving yet?"

She laughed and turned the key in the ignition. Her suitcase was packed and ready.

⚜

The next day, Jeannine, Fernández, and the Golem wore dark suits—hers with a calf-length skirt—as Curtis was laid to rest in Arlington National Cemetery. Palmer had seen to the expunging of his criminal status, allowing him to be buried next to Georgina and her brother—Jeannine's real father, Daniel.

Daniel Dufresne.

"Dufresne?" she muttered. "As in . . . "

"Yeah. The Major was Curtis's brother-in-law," whispered Fernández. "They hated each other's guts since Curtis and Georgina first dated. The Major was angry that both his sister and brother had died, while Curtis lived."

She shook her head.

After the services, Jeannine had another favor to ask of Fernández.

"David, can you watch Ollie for a few weeks?"

"Sure," said Fernández, eyeing the cat, who was on a leash and not happy about it.

"Why?"

I've learned that Daniel was my father, but there is so much still to learn. About being *me*. Not the black girl trying to be white, or the white girl trying to be black. First, I'm going to Haiti for a couple of weeks. I have a few leads the FBI passed along about my extended family. I thought I might . . . " She suddenly felt her cheeks growing hot and looked away as she let the sentence trail off.

"Want to meet them?" asked Fernández.

"Something like that, yeah," she replied.

"No problem," Fernández said. "I like the furball. And since I took Roo's old job at the cemetery to make sure the Golem can stay . . . in one piece . . . " Ollie sat up and meowed his approval.

"That's done, then," laughed Jeannine. "Let me give you some money for cat food and stuff."

"No, *señorita*. That's not necessary," said Fernández, holding up both hands.

"Didn't you know?" piped in the Golem. "That cat has plenty of money. Curtis ran a GoFundMe page for him. He said a three-legged cat would be a gold mine—and he was right. Ollie has a bigger bank account than I do."

The cat nonchalantly licked a paw and they all laughed.

Jeannine took an Uber to Dulles that evening. There were tears and hugs and promises to call and text, then she waved as the two men—one of clay, the other of flesh and blood, both now a part of her extended family—faded into the distance.

"Do you mind turning the radio on?" she asked her driver. As he did, Jeannine smiled and then asked him to turn up the volume.

It was Curtis's favorite tune—a song about Fat Tuesday that made him feel like he was home, even when halfway around the world. She took it as a good sign, and she made a promise to herself to return here to New Orleans as soon as possible.

She opened the window and felt the heat and humidity of home.

"Driver," she said. "There is an extra twenty in it for you if you step on the gas."

The engine roared and Jeannine's smile widened.

Hey now! Hey now! I-ko, I-ko, un-day.
Jock-a-mo fee-no ai na-né, jock-a-mo fee na-né.

THE END?

Not if you want to dive into more of Crystal Lake Publishing's Tales from the Darkest Depths!

Check out our amazing website and online store:
https://www.crystallakepub.com

We always have great new projects and content on the website to dive into, as well as a newsletter, behind the scenes options, social media platforms, and our very own store. If you use the IGotMyCLPBook! coupon code in the store (at the checkout), you'll get a one-time-only 50% discount on your first purchase!

We even have categories specifically for Kindle Unlimited books, non-fiction, anthologies, and others.

ACKNOWLEDGEMENTS

They say it takes a village to raise a child. It also takes a community to publish a book. *Bayou Whispers* was my MFA thesis project, so a huge thank you to the faculty, staff and administration of the Writing, Literature & Publishing department at Emerson College. A shout out to my friends and colleagues (NECONers, HWA, and ITW members) who beta-read and provided valuable feedback. To my editors Becca Borawski Jenkins and Marty Halpern who know how to kick my ass in the right direction. And to all the folks I drank with in NOLA who shared their stories, their music, and their pain with me.

Last and certainly not least, a special shout out to Joe Mynhardt and the team at Crystal Lake Publishing who took me under their wing and taught me to soar—and hugs for my wife and family who have always supported my crazy ideas. I love you all.

A lot of effort and work went into bringing my fictional world of Jeannine LaRue to you. However, any mistakes within these pages are solely my own. It is my name on the cover, after all.

R. B. Wood
Boston, April 2021

ABOUT THE AUTHOR

R. B. Wood is a recent MFA graduate of Emerson College and a writer of speculative and dark thrillers. Mr. Wood recently has appeared in Crystal Lake Publishing's *Shallow Water's* anthology, as well as online via *SickLit Magazine* & *HorrorAddicts.net,* and in the award-winning anthology *"Offbeat: Nine Spins on Song"* from Wicked Ink Books. Along with his writing passion, R. B. is the host of *The Word Count Podcast*—a show of original flash fiction.

R. B. currently lives in Boston with his partner Tina, a multitude of cats, and various other critters that visit from time to time.

Since its founding in August 2012, Crystal Lake Publishing has quickly become one of the world's leading publishers of Dark Fiction and Horror books in print, eBook, and audio formats.

While we strive to present only the highest quality fiction and entertainment, we also endeavour to support authors along their writing journey. We offer our time and experience in non-fiction projects, as well as author mentoring and services, at competitive prices.

With several Bram Stoker Award wins and many other wins and nominations, Crystal Lake Publishing puts integrity, honor, and respect at the forefront of our publishing operations.

We strive for each book and outreach program we spearhead to not only entertain and touch or comment on issues that affect our readers, but also to strengthen and support the Dark Fiction field and its authors.

Not only do we find and publish authors we believe are destined for greatness, but we strive to work with men and woman who endeavour to be decent human beings who care more for others than themselves, while still being hard working, driven, and passionate artists and storytellers.

Crystal Lake Publishing is and will always be a beacon of what passion and dedication, combined with overwhelming teamwork and respect, can accomplish. We endeavour to know each and every one of our readers, while building personal relationships with our authors, reviewers, bloggers, podcasters, bookstores, and libraries.

We will be as trustworthy, forthright, and transparent as any business can be, while also keeping most of the headaches away from our authors, since it's our job to solve the problems so they can stay in a creative mind. Which of course also means paying our authors.

We do not just publish books, we present to you worlds within your world, doors within your mind, from talented authors who sacrifice so much for a moment of your time.

There are some amazing small presses out there, and through collaboration and open forums we will continue to support other presses in the goal of helping authors and showing the world what quality small presses are capable of accomplishing. No one wins when a small press goes down, so we will always be there to support hardworking, legitimate presses and their authors. We don't see Crystal Lake as the best press out there, but we will always strive to be the best, strive to be the most interactive and grateful, and even blessed press around. No matter what happens over time, we will also take our mission very seriously while appreciating where we are and enjoying the journey.

What do we offer our authors that they can't do for themselves through self-publishing?

We are big supporters of self-publishing (especially hybrid publishing), if done with care, patience, and planning. However, not every author has the time or inclination to do market research, advertise, and set up book launch strategies. Although a lot of authors are successful in doing it all, strong small presses will always be there for the authors who just want to do what they do best: write.

What we offer is experience, industry knowledge, contacts and trust built up over years. And due to our strong brand and trusting fanbase, every Crystal Lake Publishing book comes with weight of respect. In time our fans begin to trust our judgment and will try a new author purely based on our support of said author.

With each launch we strive to fine-tune our approach, learn from our mistakes, and increase our reach. We continue to assure our authors that we're here for them and that we'll carry the weight of the launch and dealing with third parties while they focus on their strengths—be it writing, interviews, blogs, signings, etc.

We also offer several mentoring packages to authors that include knowledge and skills they can use in both traditional and self-publishing endeavours.

We look forward to launching many new careers.

This is what we believe in. What we stand for. This will be our legacy.

Welcome to Crystal Lake Publishing—Tales from the Darkest Depths

THANK YOU FOR PURCHASING THIS BOOK

CPSIA information can be obtained
at www.ICGtesting.com
Printed in the USA
LVHW051734080421
683894LV00022B/871

5/21

9 781637 529904